M000031922
THE FLIGHT
OF THE LOON
To Serenity
May you
soar.

The Flight of the Loon

One Family's Battle with Recovery

by Robert Bollendorf

ACTA Publications
Chicago, Illinois

THE FLIGHT OF THE LOON

ONE FAMILY'S BATTLE WITH RECOVERY

by Robert F. Bollendorf, Ed.D.

Edited by
Gregory F. Augustine Pierce

Typography by
Garrison Publications

Cover Design and Artwork by
Isz

Library of Congress Catalog Number: 92-074410

ISBN: 0-87946-081-4

Printed in the United States of America

Dedication

To my Family

My Wife, Children, Parents,
Brothers and Sisters
of both blood and spirit.

CHAPTER I

In many ways, that particular evening felt more like fall than spring. The still bare trees were silhouetted sharply against the sliver of red sun that flickered in the western sky. The wind had died away so completely that the lake looked like a silver platter as it mirrored the light gray sky above it. The trees reflected in the glassy water, as did the full, yellow moon swimming on a dark bank of clouds in the east. Sometimes, when the full moon shines on the waters of northern Wisconsin, it appears like so many flickering diamonds. On this night, however, it cut a smooth yellow ribbon right through the center of that silver plate.

The calm waters anticipated the loon long before it touched the surface. Its landing shattered the ribbon into golden kernels—like wheat at harvest.

Soon peace returned as the loon quietly, effortlessly glided through the stillness. Only its small wake disturbed the serenity. It was early springtime, and as yet there were no crickets or other insects to disturb the hush of the lake. Suddenly the male loon's wail cracked the silence as he summoned his mate. The haunting, half-crazed call of the loon embodied all the beauty and the loneliness of the north country.

Paul Brandt was already in his bedroom. He had excused himself early from the icy tension of the dinner table and hid in his room while his parents continued their argument. He was lying on his bed, thumbing through a bird book, attempting to ignore the yelling. He tried also to ignore the lost and scared feeling inside him. His thin face resting on his rather long, light brown hair on his pillow looked almost like a bird's in a nest. His thin, frail body barely made an impression on the mattress where he lay.

From his looks alone it was easy to tell that Paul was quiet and shy. He was the kind of kid about whom teachers would ask themselves at the end of the day, "Was Paul Brandt here today?"

It had been nearly a year since the Brandt family had confronted Paul's father, Hank, to get him to enter an alcoholism treatment center. The intervention and the subsequent treatment had been successful—at least to the extent that Hank had stayed sober ever since, as far as Paul knew. But alcohol still played a large part in their family life. Most of the arguments between Paul's mother, Molly, and Hank still seemed to start because Molly suspected Hank of stopping for a drink or because she resented him running out to AA meetings. Whatever the reason, when they argued Paul still felt like crawling into a hole to escape. His room was the next best thing.

This night, Paul and his older brother, Ryan, had agreed to open their window to let in some fresh air. The boys were alike in two ways. They both liked sleeping in a cool, almost cold room, and they had similar attitudes about cleanliness. That attitude was: "Clean only if your mother makes you." So the open window also relieved the smell of sweaty socks and underwear stashed on the floor and under the bed instead of in the clothes hamper.

Paul had probably heard the sound before on other early spring nights when the loons had stopped at the lake outside of town on their way farther north. It was in the more isolated far northern lakes with few or no motor boats that the shy birds made their summer homes and bore their young. But Paul had never really paid attention to the call before. He wasn't even sure the sound came from a bird. He asked Ryan, who was sprawled on the bed next to him, "What made that sound?"

"You should be familiar with that by now," Ryan said. "That's Mom and Dad fighting."

"Not that, Ryan!" Paul exclaimed. "The animal noise outside."

Just then the loon wailed again.

"That sound!" Paul yelled as he jumped off his bed.

"I thought you were the big bird expert," Ryan mocked. "That's a loon—just like you."

This was the first time anyone suggested that Paul and the loon were brothers. Native Americans believe that all animals are our brothers and sisters, but that we each have a special kinship with only one. Paul had always liked birds, but that night he discovered his relationship with the loon. There was something in that lonely wail that summed up all the feelings he had inside.

"What kind of bird is it?" Paul continued with Ryan.

For a change, Ryan was doing homework and began to get irritated with his younger brother. "How should I know, you bird brain. It's like a duck."

Paul began to search his bookshelf thoroughly and went through each of his many books on birds, but he couldn't find a loon.

It wasn't until the next day, when Paul checked with his science teacher, Mr. Jones, that he knew for sure that Ryan wasn't pulling his leg. Mr. Jones showed him a picture of the common loon, with its distinctive black and white markings and bright red eyes that seem to match the craziness of its call.

"You heard them last night too, eh, Paul?" Mr. Jones asked.

Paul was so enamoured with the picture of the loon that it took some time for the question to register. "Oh! Yes," he said, "I've never heard anything quite like it. How come I've never heard one before?"

"Well, the loons don't stay here. They probably just stopped on their way to their nesting grounds."

"Why don't they stay here?" Paul asked.

"Well, in a word, I guess you'd have to say 'people,'" the teacher responded. "People build cabins and beaches and destroy the marshes and tall grass where loons like to build their nests. Besides, loons are shy, nervous birds and don't like powerboats coming close to them."

Paul began to think more and more that this bird was like him. He too liked to hide out and didn't appreciate people coming close to him with their loud noises. Paul sensed in Mr. Jones the same kind of connection. The boyish looking young man with glasses too big for his face and a shy smile was a great science teacher, at least as far as Paul was concerned. Mark Jones really knew science and got excited when he spoke about the subject. But he was a timid and inexperienced teacher, and the kids knew it. So discipline in his class was a joke.

Paul once heard two teachers saying, "That's one class that won't need to visit the zoo. They're already in one!"

"Say," Mr. Jones said to Paul, "I belong to the National Preserve the Loon Club. Maybe we could start a chapter here at the school. Would you be interested?"

"Sure," Paul answered. "But why do they need to be protected? Are they endangered?"

"Once there were loons throughout the northern states," Mr. Jones replied sadly, "but now only Minnesota has them in abundance."

"What would our club do?" Paul asked.

"Well, as a project we could fix up a nesting site on the lake outside of town and see if we couldn't entice two loons to stay here this spring. Then we would have to guard the nest to keep powerboats away from it."

The thought of having the wonderful cry of the loon coming through his open window all summer long inspired Paul. "Let's do it!" he declared with uncharacteristic decisiveness. "How do we start?"

"Well," said Mr. Jones excitedly, "talk to your friends. Let's see if we can generate some more interest."

Paul's shoulders sagged. He didn't have many friends in the junior high, and he certainly didn't see himself as a leader. As a child, Paul had always been painfully shy, and, while he had made progress in his "social skills" the year since his dad had quit drinking, he was still reluctant to set himself up for rejection.

Yet Paul usually found alternatives to being outgoing, and this situation was no exception.

"How about if I make some posters and then you announce the club in class, Mr. Jones?"

"That sounds fine Paul," the teacher said gently, for he understood what the earnest young man was struggling with. "Now you better run so you don't miss the bus."

"O.K.," Paul agreed. "See you tomorrow." The teacher grinned as he watched the boy careen down the hallway.

The next day Paul came with his signs and Mr. Jones made his announcement in class. The response was less enthusiastic than they both had hoped, but it was about what they should have expected. Only three other kids joined—all loners, like Paul. The three probably joined more to identify with something or someone than from a real commitment to saving loons. Nor was the membership likely to increase, since the club quickly became known around the school as "the Loonies."

Undaunted by their reputation, however, the club members began their mission the following weekend when they visited the lake and walked around the shore looking for the best possible nesting site for a pair of loons.

CHAPTER II

It doesn't take long for word about unusual behavior to spread through a small town. Soon everyone knew about the Loonies. Most folks just smiled. A few school board members, however, were angry that one of their teachers had become the subject of ridicule. A few people even supported the efforts of Paul and his friends, although they did so silently.

Around the Brandt kitchen table, the Loonies provoked new arguments—ones, at least, that involved new participants and weren't about alcohol or AA meetings.

"Even though you're still in junior high, we've already heard the whole story at the high school," Ryan complained to Paul. "I don't like being ridiculed because of you and your stupid loons."

Paul sat quietly staring at the floor while his brother continued. "You know, me and my friends go to the lake all the time to go boating and swimming. I'm already dreading the warm weather. We'll go to the beach and there you'll be with your geek friends doing God knows what with some goofy looking birds."

"That goes double for me," their sister Sally added. "Word travels fast in grade school, too, and it's twice as hard to get people to like you when your older brother is being made fun of. Someone called me a 'loon balloon' the other day."

"Oh lighten up, you two!" Bobbie, the elder sister protested. "I think it's neat that Paul's excited about something. Your precious popularity will survive."

"That's easy for you to say, Bobbie," Ryan countered. "You're graduating in a few weeks. Me, I have to return to that school in the fall."

Hank leaned back in his chair and spoke for the first time.

"Well, Molly," he said, "you claim I'm not recovering, but look at me! Right now I'm doing all I can to 'let go and let God' instead of jumping in and ending this argument."

"Hank, when it comes to these kids you've been letting go since they were babies," Molly shot back sarcastically.

The kids all looked quickly over at Hank. He just smiled, and the tension was relieved—for now, at least.

About a week later came the first really warm day of spring. The water in the lake was still far too cold for swimming, but the sun was bright. As it baked the sand, it seemed ready and waiting to thaw bones chilled by the long winter.

Ryan and his friends staked out their usual headquarters on the shore at the Roper place. John Roper's father was a prominent attorney and school board member, and his mother ran the clothing store in town. John was their only child and they spoiled him terribly. The Ropers lived on the lake, and they had a private beach where they docked a huge speedboat. The teenage boys liked the spot, because they weren't subject to the rules of the public beach next door. Yet only a small fence separated them from it, so they could still conveniently check out the girls.

That morning, the band of high schoolers worked hard to put the Roper's dock in the water and to launch the boat for the season. Both of John's parents were away at meetings, so the boys had also downed a few beers. Now that their work was finished, they were lying on the dock and entertaining themselves by commenting on which of the girls sunbathing on the beach had picked up a few pounds over the winter. They also had great fun at the expense of the Loonies, who were out in a small dinghy trying to anchor some buoys. As was usually the case, John Roper lead the assault.

Roper—which is what everyone called him—was quite large. He looked like he might be a linebacker on the football team, but in fact most of his afternoons during the school year were spent in detentions. Roper had short, cropped black hair, piercing brown eyes and a pockmarked face that completed his linebacker appearance.

Mark Jones was supervising the Loonies as they carefully tried to drop anchors that would secure the buoys, each buoy carrying a sign reading: "Loon Preserve. No Wake."

Roper commented to Ryan, "Maybe when Paul gets done with his loon posters, he can come over to the beach and post a 'Save the Whale' sign for when your sister Sally goes swimming."

"Button it, Roper. Don't even mention those two to me," Ryan replied. Ryan was smaller than Roper, but like most of the Brandt males, except for Paul, he had an athletic looking body, which had developed considerably over the last year. Ryan had a rugged strength that his friends respected. He would talk tough, just like Roper, but there was rarely any menace in his words.

"Roper, you're just bitter because some girl who has yet to lose her baby fat has probably spurned your pitiful advances," Zack said playfully.

Zack Pierce was Ryan's best friend. They had been friends since grade school. There was a time when Zack would have been right in the middle of the ridicule of others and involved in the beer drinking. But that was before he had been arrested for driving under the influence of alcohol and his parents had forced him to get help for what he admitted had become a problem. In spite of Zack's early resentment at being confronted with being an alcoholic at such a young age, the treatment had "taken hold" and he was staying sober. In conversations with Ryan, Zack credited the addictions treatment center at the local hospital and Alcoholics Anonymous with turning his life around.

Zack was now a member of the swim team and very conscientious about school. In many ways he no longer fit in with this particular group, and he probably wouldn't hang out with them if Ryan wasn't there. Zack avoided situations where there was drinking unless, like today, there was plenty of open space and other activities for him to be involved in. Since he had quit drinking alcohol and using drugs,

Zack's surfer boy face had taken on a peaceful and gentle appearance that matched his new personality. But he remained one person who was not intimidated by Roper.

"Oh Zack, I forgot you were here," Roper said in mock contrition. "I guess it's because you never have diddly to say until someone says something critical of one of the Brandts." Roper tried to sound as playful as Zack, but the tension in their relationship rose icily to the surface.

"We never have to worry about forgetting you're around, do we Roper?" Zack fired back.

"Hey, we did all this work getting the boat in the water," said Steve Johnson, another one of the gang of boys, changing the subject. "Are we ever going to take it out, or are we going to lie on this beach listening to you guys bicker all afternoon?"

"Yeah!" Roper yelled. "Let's go swamp the Loonies."

Few people got as much enjoyment out of disturbing other people as did John Roper.

He raced down the dock and jumped into the boat. The others followed with much less enthusiasm. When they were aboard, Roper started the powerful inboard motor and quickly backed out of the dock, heading for the other side of the lake where the Loonies were setting the buoys.

Paul, along with Mark Jones and two other members of the club, were struggling in a small dinghy with the heavy anchors that would hold the buoys in place. The ice had melted off the lake only a few weeks earlier, so none of them were anxious to get wet.

They were leaning over the edge, putting in one of the anchors, when Roper's big inboard went speeding by not five feet from them. In a moment, they were all in the cold water. As Paul found himself struggling to the surface, the first thing he felt was a band tightening around his chest—his muscles constricting from the cold. Paul wasn't sure he'd be able to breathe even if he made it to the surface. When he finally broke the water, the others were already up and swimming the short distance to shore. Mr. Jones turned to see if Paul was all right.

"Can you swim?" he managed to ask.

"I think so," Paul said, gasping for air.

Luckily for the freezing Loonies, the day had started out cool but had gradually warmed. They had each started the day in long pants and sweatshirts but had peeled off layers of clothes. By the time they had been dumped overboard they were all in shorts and tee shirts. Now they were able to take off their wet clothes and replace them with dry, warm ones. The spring sun and the dry clothes soon helped their shivering to subside. Nothing helped their sense of humiliation and frustration.

Roper slowed the boat long enough to make sure each of the Loonies made it to shore safely, then he laughed and sped toward the public beach.

"Smart move, Roper," Zack yelled sarcastically. "There was a teacher in that boat. Are you looking to get expelled?"

"You mean Jones, the king of the Loonies and the wimps?" Roper replied. "He wouldn't report us even if it had happened in school—which it didn't. The Loonies are not a school-sponsored club. My dad would just love to have an excuse to get rid of that jerk. Just let him try to make trouble. He and that club are an embarrassment to the school and this town. We just did everyone a favor."

"Wow! Look." Steve again redirected the conversation. "Michelle got a new bikini over the winter. Let's get a closer look. Swing by the beach."

Ryan was noticeably quiet. He hoped that this experience would get Paul off his loon kick, but he also hoped Paul wouldn't go home and tell Hank. His father always seemed to be just waiting for an excuse to jump on Ryan's case.

"Hey, Michelle. How about a ride?" Roper yelled

toward the beach. She ignored him, as she always did.

Meanwhile Paul sat on the shore, still shivering every once in a while. "Those guys are in trouble now," he exclaimed. "What are you going to do to them, Mr. Jones?"

"Nothing," the teacher answered quietly.

"But Mr. Jones, we could have drowned out there!" Paul stammered.

"I know, Paul, and it was a very stupid thing for them to do," Mr. Jones responded gently. "But to make an issue of it would only cause more ridicule for what we're trying to do. Do you want that?"

"No, but . . ." Paul paused. He wanted to say more, but he gave in to Mr. Jones's superior logic. Paul was confused. Sometimes, he thought, grown-ups can make things sound right even when they don't seem right.

Paul decided that he wouldn't say anything at home, either. If he did, his dad would just yell at Ryan as usual. It would end with the whole family being mad at Paul for causing trouble.

He'd just have to get even with Ryan by making him wonder whether or not he'd tell. Since Ryan was used to being in trouble, however, Paul wasn't sure how effective that tactic would be.

All this scheming just made his head hurt. It was bad enough being cold, without having a headache too.

CHAPTER III

Sally was sunbathing with her friends on the public beach and had watched as Roper swamped the Loonies. She let out a gasp as she saw Paul thrown into the water, but once she saw him reach shore safely, she joined in the laughter with all her friends. Their delight increased as they watched the big speedboat head toward them. The young girls, just entering adolescence, thought high school boys were gods, and Sally thought John Roper, with all his confidence and power, was the best.

Though the water was still quite cold, her excitement and her few pounds of extra insulation allowed her to wade out past her knees to welcome the boys like a tropical island girl whose men had just returned from a long, successful fishing venture. The boys, though, were concentrating on Michelle Lawrence in her new bathing suit and hardly noticed Sally until they realized that Michelle was snubbing them.

Things had changed for Sally in the past year, not so much because of the intervention with Sally's father and his stopping drinking, but just because she was reaching the age when things change quickly for young girls. In the Brandt family, she was still the joker who often had everyone bending over in laughter, and she brought that same skill to her friendships. Sally had lots of friends, and because she was funny, the other girls enjoyed being around her. That had always been true. What was changing were the bodies of those friends—that, and the fact that the subject of boys crept more and more into their endless phone conversations. Boys were suddenly the main focus of the girls' pointing and giggling during school and their long exchanges while walking home and sitting on each others' porches.

But Sally's body was not changing—at least not as far as she could tell. It was still the cute little round body that seemed to fit so well with her comedian personality but not at all with the prospect of attracting a boy's attention.

The only boy Sally felt totally comfortable with was Paul. Though they were very different—or maybe because of that—they had always been close. Sally had always made fun of her brother, and, no matter how biting the humor, he always just smiled. If they were alone, the two talked easily, and Paul often had interesting things to say, though she rarely told him that.

The other day, for example, Paul had said he noticed that, though she could still make people laugh, more and more often her jokes seemed to be at her own expense. He said she was drawing attention to herself as a defense against her own pain. That night at a sleepover with friends, Sally had looked at herself in the mirror in front of the others, raised her wrist to her forehead and sighed, "Puberty has passed me by." That got a laugh out of her friends, but Paul's words rang in her ears.

Sally was at a point in her life when her fat was no longer just baby fat. It was fat. Even though she wasn't very overweight, next to her taller, slimmer friends she stood out. Though she didn't let on, she hated being the "perky, pudgy" one.

Among the Brandt family, sensitive issues were discussed, but never honestly or directly. Everything was fair game—especially where Sally was concerned—as long as it was in the form of a joke.

So as the speedboat went by her, it was natural for Ryan and his friends to shout "Whale off the starboard bow. Man the harpoons!"

Then they all laughed. Sally, being ever quick to join in, scooped up some of the cold water and sucked it into her mouth, blowing it out like a whale uses its blow hole. The boys and her friends laughed all the louder.

When Paul and Sally met on the way home from the lake that afternoon, they both walked quietly for a while. Finally, Sally spoke.

"So, will you give up on this silly project of yours now, Paul?" she asked.

"No way, Sally," Paul shot back with a fierceness contrary to his nature. "If it's so embarrassing to you to have me protect a few helpless birds, you'll just have to live with it."

"I'm sorry, Paul," she said. "Actually, it's me I find most embarrassing right now, and I need your help with it."

"What do you mean, Sally?" Paul asked. "You're confusing me."

Sally went on to describe what had happened at the beach, and how the boys' words and laughter had felt like real harpoons, and how each had hurt her deeply. She then went on to describe her plan for losing weight.

"I'm going to join the track team at school. That

way I won't have to eat dinner with the rest of the family. I'll tell Mom to save me just a salad because my stomach is all jumbled from running. I'll tell her I'm eating a big lunch at school and I'm not that hungry at dinner."

"Why can't you just go on a regular diet or just eat less?" Paul asked.

"Because Mom thinks I'm too young for diets, and besides they don't work for me. Once I start to eat I have trouble stopping. The only thing that works for me is to skip meals." Sally's voice sounded more and more pleading.

"Paul, would you get up and run with me in the morning?" she asked. "I can tell Mom I need to do it for track and that you're going with me to keep me company and for the exercise."

"Oh, Sally, I hate running!" Paul whined. "I use any excuse I can to get out of it in gym class."

"Please, Paul! I know I won't get up on my own, but with your help I could do it." Sally grabbed his arm and raised her right hand for emphasis. "I promise I won't bug you about the loons and I'll even stick up for you against Ryan."

"I don't think Ryan will say much anyway," Paul replied wryly. "He knows if he does I'll tell Dad what happened today and that they were drinking to boot."

"Will you do it for me, Paul?" Sally begged.

"O.K.," Paul finally conceded, "but only till you're in the habit and can do it on your own. And you have to promise not to tell Mom and Dad what happened today."

Neither Sally nor Paul said a word at dinner that night about the dunking, and Ryan spent the night waiting for the shoe that never dropped. Paul avoided Ryan and didn't even look at his brother during dinner, which seemed to bug Ryan more than usual.

Paul felt good about giving his brother the silent treatment, although that night he had bad dreams that all involved not being able to breathe.

So he wasn't sorry when morning came, even though it meant he had to keep his promise to Sally to go running. It was cold, and Paul complained the entire time it took them to go around the block twice. Sally had to stop and walk a lot, which didn't bother Paul at all. She tried to talk him into a third trip, but it had turned even colder and Paul said, "I'm going in."

"At least we did it," she said as she followed him inside.

CHAPTER IV

Despite the abuse they received from people in school and the town, the Loonies persisted in their attempts to establish a nesting site. Maybe it was because, for kids used to being totally ignored, negative attention was better than none at all. Or perhaps it was because they soon saw their efforts rewarded. A pair of loons nested on the lake.

The Loonies took turns watching the birds. During one of Paul's watches, the female loon laid an egg in the nest. Paul felt as though he were a part of the family—an older brother maybe. He began coming to the nesting site even when it wasn't his turn to observe.

It was on one of his regular days, a Saturday, that it happened. It was a cloudy day, but warm and humid. Paul had gotten tired of lying on his stomach watching the loons through the binoculars and had rolled over onto his back. He didn't need to watch them constantly. He had learned to tell what was happening from their different calls. At the moment, the female was sitting on the nest while the male was out fishing. They communicated back and forth with short, soft, little calls that sounded like hoots.

Then Paul heard the male use the tremolo—the laughing sound that loons make when they are frightened. As soon as he rolled over, he saw why.

Roper's speedboat was heading straight towards the loon. It quickly dove to avoid the boat and to divert it from the nest. The tactic worked momentarily as Roper slowed down to see where the loon had gone.

Roper had ignored the "No Wake" signs and had charged the male at full speed. The wake from the boat began to wash up on shore. Loons, though very agile in water, are clumsy on land. With legs far back on their bodies, they are great divers but terrible walkers. Because of this, they build their nests right at the edge of the water, and the wake from passing speedboats disturbs them greatly.

As the wake began splashing the nest, the female waddled into the water and began flapping her wings and running on the surface of the water until she had enough speed to get airborne. She then flew away from Roper's boat—partly from fear but also to lead the intruder away from the nest.

The male loon finally surfaced out near the middle of the lake and Roper and his friends quickly gave chase. Having accomplished his diversion mission and having the room this time he needed for his long take-off, the male also took flight. Paul watched as the male skimmed the water with the speedboat closing in. The bird gained altitude before the boat could catch him.

Paul turned his attention back toward the nest, but he was too late. The damage had been done. The chick would not be born. A gull had landed in the unprotected nest, pecked a hole in the shell and was now greedily devouring the insides. Paul screamed and waved his arms, but it was in vain.

The male and female returned to the nest at the same time. Paul heard their familiar wail for what he thought would be the last time that summer. It sounded sadder and lonelier than ever, but perhaps that was because it echoed his own feelings as tears streamed down his cheeks.

Paul was not the only one who observed the boat chasing the loons. Ryan had been lying on Roper's dock and watched as the boat had sped inside the buoys. He had seen his brother stand up in the weeds and wave his arms, but he didn't know why. Roper and the boys in the boat knew only that they had scared the male bird.

Paul wanted to walk over to Roper's house and confront them all. He had even picked up a stick to use to make his point. As he got closer, however, he saw the boys pop the tops on cans of beer as they climbed laughing from the boat. The sound of the cans opening brought back the dread that Paul used to feel when his father would open a beer in the middle of a tirade. Suddenly Paul's rage turned to fear and he stopped in his tracks.

He returned to the loon sight to find Mark Jones staring into the nest. Through his clenched teeth Paul told his teacher the whole story.

"Well, maybe it's for the best," Mr. Jones said sadly. "It's still early. The loons can still fly to a new nesting site and still have a chick yet this year. Maybe loons don't belong on this lake. It's just too busy."

"But I want them on this lake!" Paul shouted.

Mark Jones smiled. He liked this intense young man. "Loons and people don't mix, Paul," he said. His voice was calm.

"We don't get along with people either, but we can't just fly away," Paul fired back. He didn't even notice he had said "we," but Mr. Jones did.

"Perhaps we can learn from the loon to accept that there are battles we just can't win," Mr. Jones answered in the same gentle voice. "The loon has survived for millions of years. Perhaps that's one reason. It knows when to retreat."

"I don't want to survive if I have to spend my life retreating," Paul said angrily.

He ran home, leaving Mark Jones to decide what to do with the egg that would never hatch. Paul went straight to his room, knowing Ryan would be home soon. He waited behind the door.

CHAPTER V

Ryan left for home shortly after Paul. "Stick around and have another beer," Roper said. "We'll wait for the loons to settle down again, then we'll take another shot at them."

"No, I'd better get home and stay in good with my old man so I can go out tonight," Ryan answered.

"Why not just stay here and drink right through dinner? Then you'll already be out and your old man can't make you stay home." This was Roper's logic after several beers.

"But once I did get home, he might keep me there all summer," Ryan tried uselessly to reason.

"You've become a real worrier, Brandt," Roper answered. "You don't drink as much, you hardly ever get detentions anymore, and I end up sitting in the dean's office by myself. You've become almost as big a wimp as your friend Zack. Next, you'll be joining the Pep Club at school."

To add to his embarrassment, Ryan had to get on his bike and pedal home. He had a driver's license, but his sister and mother were using the second car that afternoon.

"Now be careful with your bike in traffic," he heard Roper mock as he rode away.

When Ryan got home, he went directly to his room, afraid that his mother might smell the beer on his breath. When he walked through the door, Paul sprang at him. His agile little body felt more like a distracting insect to Ryan than the mountain lion Paul wished he were. He didn't even knock Ryan down. Ryan simply bent his back and gave a little twist and it was Paul who landed on the floor. He tried to struggle to his feet, but Ryan was quickly on top of him. Ryan pinned down Paul's arms and legs.

Ryan's voice was angry, but he spoke in hushed tones so as not to attract his mother's attention. "What's the matter with you, you little jerk?"

Paul didn't try to be so quiet. "You killed the . . ."

Ryan quickly covered Paul's mouth.

"Shut up!"

Their mother was quick to detect the sharp voices,

even from downstairs.

"What's going on up there?" Molly called from the bottom of the stairs.

"Nothing," Ryan managed to answer calmly. "I just tripped on some junk by the door."

"Maybe you should clean that pigsty so you don't kill yourself," Molly called, returning to her work in the kitchen.

Ryan whispered closely into Paul's ear, "I'll take my hand from your mouth, if you promise to talk quietly."

Paul tried to bite the hand, but Ryan held his mouth shut. Then, though he wanted so much to continue being strong, Paul began to cry in spite of himself.

When Ryan slowly took his hand from Paul's mouth, Paul whispered angrily, "You killed the chick."

"What are you talking about?" Ryan asked, genuinely confused. "I wasn't even in the boat. Besides, they never went near the nest."

"The wake from the boat scared away the mother. While she was gone, a seagull ate the egg. You might as well have gone over and stepped on it," Paul sobbed, as again his tears betrayed him.

"I'm sorry, Paul. Really I am. But how were they supposed to know that would happen?" Ryan's voice sounded sincere.

"They didn't have to know," Paul blurted, the words tripping over each other in his anger. "All they had to do was obey the stupid 'No Wake' signs and let the loons alone. What had they done to anybody? What had we done to anybody? Now their baby's dead and they'll leave for sure."

Paul forgot about his mother and screamed, "I hope you're all happy!"

Ryan again covered his brother's mouth. "I didn't like the club, Paul. I admit it. But I'm sorry about the egg," he said. Ryan's voice again sounded sympathetic. "I know you're mad at me because they're my friends, but I wasn't even in the boat. What did you expect me to do?" He took his hand away again.

"Even if you were with them you wouldn't have stopped them," Paul sniffed. "I didn't see you throwing yourself overboard to stop them when they swamped us a few weeks back."

"You're right, I probably wouldn't have," Ryan admitted. "And I appreciate the fact that you didn't tell Dad. But Paul, why do you have to get so upset about some stupid birds?" Ryan sounded truly confused.

"Why do you care about such stupid friends?" Paul responded.

It was an impasse and they both knew it. "O.K.," Ryan answered. "I'll say it again, I'm sorry it happened. If I let you up, do you promise not to tell Mom or Dad?"

"Yeah," Paul said. "But just stay away from me and keep your freaking friends away, too. Better yet, put them in a cage somewhere."

Ryan wanted to laugh and rub his knuckles through Paul's hair, but he thought better of it. He was pretty sure Paul knew they had been drinking at Roper's house, and he didn't want to upset Paul enough to tell their parents. He let Paul up and walked out of the room, respecting his brother's desire to be left alone.

After the egg was destroyed, the rest of the club gave up on the loons. Paul continued to work on the site, hoping the loons would stay, or at least come back the next year.

Mr. Jones took the empty egg to science class to show why people shouldn't make a wake near a loon's nest, but that just gave his students another reason to make fun of him and the Loonies.

The last act of the club, led by Paul, was to steal the egg from the classroom and bury it near the nesting site. They put a cross on it with the inscription:

"Here's a life that will never be,
due to John Roper's stupidity."

But they hid the grave in the weeds and wrote small, because they were afraid Roper might find it.

CHAPTER VI

It was the first anniversary of Hank's sobriety. He had had one little bracer that Molly didn't know about before going to see the counselor the day of the intervention. That had been his last drink.

Hank stopped at the hardware store on his way home from work to pick up some things he needed for a project Molly had been bugging him to finish. He met up with someone he knew from AA, and they decided to go to the bakery for a cup of coffee and a sweet roll to celebrate Hank's anniversary. Hank got home a few minutes late, and he could tell that Molly was tense, although she tried to ask pleasantly where he had been.

Sarcastically, Hank replied, "I stopped by the bar and had a few drinks to celebrate my one year of sobriety, Nosey. I wanted to accept my medallion at the meeting tonight with a buzz on."

"I was just asking, Hank," Molly said defensively.

"Yeah, yeah, I know," Hank said sadly. "And you have no business asking. God, Molly, it's been a year. When are you going to let it go?"

"Hank, for ten years I waited almost every night with a house full of kids not knowing where you were or when you'd get home," Molly replied with a combination of anger and sadness in her voice. "So you'll have to excuse me if I have a little problem forgetting. I do my best."

"How long are you going to make me suffer for those things I can't change, Molly?" he replied with his own mixed feelings of anger and hopelessness. "Do you have any idea how hard each day is?"

Hank went off to read the paper and settle down before dinner, while Molly finished preparing it. She had made his favorite meal and even a little cake with one candle to celebrate. Sally had started track practice and wouldn't be home for dinner, and Ryan had a part-time job at the supermarket. The oldest son, Scott, was away at college, so it was just Hank, Molly, Bobbie and Paul who sat down at the dinner table.

Paul wished Sally were there to crack a few jokes to ease the tension. When Hank saw the dinner and the cake, however, he kissed Molly on the cheek and said, "Thanks, Moll," and a pleasant conversation followed. After the meal they ate cake and sang "Happy Anniversary to You." Hank seemed to Paul to be nervous but appreciative of the fuss.

They had finished the cake when Bobbie asked the question only she could get away with, "Daddy, what has it been like for you the last year?"

Hank sat back in his chair for a moment. Paul thought his father seemed surprised at the candor of the question, but he also seemed lost in thought. Paul's first impulse was to excuse himself, but his curiosity for once overruled his fear of conflict.

"Well, I'm going to an AA meeting tonight, and my sponsor is going to present me with my one-year medallion," he finally responded, "I'm proud of that, but it is the first time in a while that I have looked forward to going to a meeting. It seems too seldom that people get recognized at a meeting for doing good things. People in AA always seem to focus on their problems. All I seem to hear about is either problems getting sober or problems staying sober, and I'm tired of problems. Life never seems to be much fun anymore."

"To tell you the truth," Hank continued, "I don't miss the taste of alcohol. My craving for alcohol seemed to disappear after a month or so. But I find myself more and more forgetting the bad times that alcohol caused and remembering more and more the good times. My sponsor tells me that this too shall pass and to just keep going to meetings, but I'm getting pretty tired of them."

Paul thought how nice it was to hear his dad talk quietly about things rather than yell about them like he always used to.

"You seemed real excited when you first got out of treatment, Dad." Paul couldn't believe he had made such a direct observation about his father's recovery. The ease of his Dad's response was even more surprising to him.

"Oh, yeah, when I left treatment I was really gung ho for sobriety and for going to meetings," Hank replied with a laugh. "I got a sponsor while I was still in the treatment center, and I would talk to him daily on the telephone. Now, me and your mother fight about me going to another meeting like we used to fight about me going to the bar."

Molly started to react but then thought better of it. "The honeymoon is over, I guess," Hank continued. "It seems to me that having a sponsor is like having a second wife: 'Did you get to a meeting?' 'Have you had quiet time today?' 'How are you coming on your fourth step?' I have a wife to nag me, I don't need a sponsor too!"

"But Hank, what do you want from me?" Molly

had contained herself as long as she could. "Can't you accept that your life has changed and these are things you need to do to make it successful?"

"First of all, Molly, I can't believe you're asking me that, when you don't accept the things you need to do to make your own life successful." Hank shot back. Molly picked up some dishes and went to the sink. Everyone fell silent.

Finally, Hank changed the subject. "To tell you the truth, Bobbie, I'd like to be able to drink socially like so many other people do, and I resent people who seem to be able to do so. My brother, Ken, for instance, can stop at a bar now and then with the guys from the construction company and have a few beers. He always makes excuses for me because we both know I can't join him. Even if I told myself I would only drink a soda, in my heart I know better. Once at the bar, it would be like old times and I know that with all the other guys sitting around drinking beer, I would want one too."

Molly's face turned ashen, but she continued to listen. "So I drive home or go to a meeting instead," Hank said, "but I miss going out with the guys I work with. People at the meetings laugh and joke, but it's not the same. In all honesty, what I miss most is that simply by bending my elbow and putting a cold beer to my mouth I could end all my cares and feel on top of the world. When I was in a bar the tensions of the day disappeared—literally. They just floated away."

Molly kept clearing the table. She was visibly agitated. Paul and Bobbie sat riveted to their chairs. They had never heard their father talk this way.

"Then there is the problem with feelings," he went on. "Everyone is always wanting to know how I feel. I drank so I wouldn't have to know how I felt. Now, everyone wants to know about my feelings. Then when I do take the time to check how I'm feeling, I find I am usually depressed, lonely or angry. So what's the use of knowing?"

Now it was Molly's turn to speak. She came up behind her husband and put her hands on his shoulders. "You know, Hank, this is the first time in a year that we've really talked openly about this kind of thing," she said gently. "I don't like everything I hear, but I can handle it. Maybe I can even help. Why don't you let me in more?"

"It seems to me you don't want to just know," Hank replied steadily. "You want to control. When Bobbie asked me about this past year, I heard concern and interest. When you ask, I hear meddling and accusation."

"Hank, for years I was home with little kids and no one to talk to," Molly began, leaving her hands where they were.

Hank rolled his eyes, thinking he'd heard this

speech before, but it took a new twist.

"I so much enjoyed it early in our marriage when you would come home from work, and we'd talk and I'd tell you about cute little things the kids did," Molly said. "Then, when you started coming home later and later, my disappointment turned to anger. Then we'd fight, and that was the last thing I wanted. Now, even though the kids are big and I have lots of people to talk to, I still look forward to seeing my husband walk through the back door. Since you've quit drinking I've discovered a new feeling when you don't come home. I feel rejected."

Hank was silent for a while. "How do things get so screwed up, Molly?" he asked gently. "You were always my favorite person to talk to, too." He smiled and took her hand. "I'd like it to be that way again."

"I'll try harder, Hank," Molly said, sitting down next to him and looking into his eyes for the first time in a long time.

"So will I," he answered tenderly.

Paul and Bobbie slipped from the room.

CHAPTER VII

Though Molly and Pastor Brooks had been acquainted for many years, it was through their mutual friend, Dr. Joshua Krueger, that they had become real friends. Josh had been a quiet man who loved music. Besides being the town's doctor, he had also been the song leader for the pastor and Molly's congregation. His courage in facing his own illness and death had helped give Molly the strength she needed to go through with Hank's intervention and had led Pastor Brooks to change his own life radically.

Josh Krueger's love for music was truly contagious. After Josh's death, the pastor had appointed Molly the church's music director and become her assistant. Although he didn't have Josh's sweet tenor voice, he could still carry a tune. And nothing helped him express his feelings more fully than music.

All his adult life, John Brooks had been a man who lived through his intellect. His mind was not in the clouds, it was in the heavens. He had looked down on people with a distant curiosity and provided only a sterile spirituality to the parishioners who brought him the problems of their lives.

But Josh Krueger had changed all that. He had talked openly with his pastor—indeed the entire congregation—about his illness and coming death, sharing his fears and his regrets. Josh's openness enabled his friend to become more aware of his own feelings. These feelings started with the pastor's own loneliness and fear, but then became true empathy for the people who came to him for guidance. While he never lost his intellectual curiosity, his focus changed. He began to read books about people and how to help them. He studied counseling and psychology. He became interested in 12-step programs like Alcoholics Anonymous and Al-Anon in which many of his parishioners participated. He even began to attend those groups' open public information meetings to learn more directly what they had to offer.

Over the past year following Josh's death, Pastor Brooks had gradually taken over the role of Molly's friend and confidant that had previously been Josh's. In Pastor Brooks, Molly found a person who was not only understanding but excited about the intervention with her husband she had organized and the changes that had followed.

After the scene on Hank's anniversary, and with Pastor Brook's encouragement, Molly again committed herself to change.

"Each day, I tell myself I'll be different," Molly confided to the minister as she sat at the organ while they practiced the hymns for that coming Sunday. "I really thought that after the intervention life would be easy. I never expected this. I hear 'Let go and let God' in Al-Anon all the time, but all the silly slogans don't make it happen. I've tried, but I can't let go."

"Molly, that saying is just talking about the same faith in God that you've been encouraged to have ever since you were a child in religion class," Pastor Brooks replied. "You are being asked to believe that God has a plan for you. Your job is to accept and follow the plan, not manufacture it."

"O.K., then, what about the expression, 'Pray as if everything depended on God and act as if everything depended on you'?" Molly challenged.

"That's still good theology, Molly, but you're overdoing the last part," the pastor replied. "You're trying to act for Hank, not just yourself, and you can't do that."

"My head understands, John. I just wish I could convince my heart," Molly relented. "Do you think God will forgive me for what I'm doing to my husband and family?"

"Forgive you for what?" Pastor Brooks asked. "For loving them too much? For wanting the best for them and trying to make it happen?"

Molly sat silently for a few minutes. Then she stood abruptly and started for the church door.

"Tonight, I'm going to bring back the love and romance that was once present in our marriage," she announced with an uncharacteristic giggle. "I think a little party for two is in order to celebrate a year of recovery."

"Well, don't expect too much from one night, Molly," her friend warned. "Your problems didn't start in one night, and they probably won't end that quickly, either."

But Molly didn't seem to hear. She left quickly as though she were on a mission.

That night was a Friday, and Paul ate dinner alone. Molly and Hank had eaten early so Hank could get to a meeting, and the other children were all out at friends' houses for the night. After he had eaten, Paul was anxious to take advantage of the fact that he practically had the bathroom to himself. With five kids and only one bathroom, no one in the Brandt family had the luxury of taking much time in the bathroom—except at rare times like these. His mom was home, but she always took showers and was in and out in no time. So when Paul found the door locked, he waited outside, confident she'd be right out. When he heard water running into the tub—the sound of someone taking a bath—he knocked on the door. "Sally, is that you?" Paul called quizzically.

"No," Molly answered. "It's your mother."

"Will you be out soon?" Paul asked, surprised.

"I'll probably be a while," Molly answered.

Paul walked away feeling confused as well as uncomfortable.

After her bath, Molly powdered her body and put on her makeup. Then she took a long look at herself in the mirror. She saw a woman who was remarkably resilient, considering she had had five children and was over forty. But a longer, closer look told the rest of the story. She saw lines, sagging skin and varicose veins. Molly shrugged. She liked her body. Besides, she had earned every wrinkle.

She put on the negligee she found in the bottom of her dresser drawer and the long lacy robe that went over it. When Paul walked by her after she finally opened the bathroom door he was sure he was seeing a mirage. But enough reality sunk in for him to know he should make himself scarce.

On his way back from the bathroom, Paul could see his mother reading in the living room. He became curious how his dad would react. The AA meeting had started at 7:30 and usually lasted an hour, so Paul began listening for him at about 9:00. By 9:30, when Hank still wasn't home, he could hear his mother begin to rustle the pages of her book, and he heard the long sighs that usually signalled aggravation. At 10:30, he heard her heading up the stairs to bed, even though he knew she wouldn't sleep.

Molly had just turned out the bedroom lights when Hank walked in. "Another celebration?" she spat out, not even trying to hide her irritation. Paul felt guilty for listening through the bedroom wall, but curiosity got the best of him.

Hank sounded surprised. "Molly! I expected you to be in bed. I didn't realize you'd be waiting up for me. I thought the kids . . ."

She quickly walked over to him and gently put her hand to his mouth.

"I'm sorry I snapped, Hank," she whispered. I didn't want it to be this way. Let's go to bed. Paul's asleep, and the others are staying with friends."

Paul shut his eyes tight. He had invaded their privacy and didn't want to hear the sounds from his parents' bedroom. For a while, everything was quiet, but all too soon he heard a noise he didn't expect. He heard the bedroom door opening and his father's frustrated voice saying, "Now there's nothing between us that works anymore!" Then Paul heard the door slam.

Then from the bedroom he heard his mother's sad voice calling, "I shouldn't have rushed you, Hank. It's O.K. It'll be better next time."

In his heart, Paul knew it really wasn't O.K. Things were not fine, and they certainly wouldn't get better tonight nor tomorrow. He began to wonder about ever.

CHAPTER VIII

As he looked back on the days that followed, Paul was convinced that it was God's will that kept the loons on the same site and that allowed the mother loon to lay not one but two more eggs. It must also have been God that put the praying mantises where he and Mark Jones could observe them.

Paul was at the loon site with his teacher on the day after the incident in his parents' bedroom. Paul was tired. He hadn't gotten much sleep the night before. He had never given sex much thought. It wasn't that he didn't know the facts of life. He knew where those two eggs came from that the mother and father loon guarded so closely. He had watched birds and other animals mate. It always seemed so natural. But humans were complicated. They didn't have sex just during mating season. His brother Ryan seemed to be in constant heat, judging from the way he talked about girls and how he looked at the magazines he smuggled into their room. How could humans take such a simple, natural thing and mess it up so badly?

Paul watched a girl water-skiing in the middle of the lake. She wore a bikini and was pleasant enough to look at, but he didn't get the urges that Ryan talked about. He wondered if he ever would—or if he wanted to after hearing what he had the night before. Paul had the feeling that something had gone very wrong for his parents, but he couldn't understand how they could fail at expressing love.

"You seem preoccupied today, Paul," Mr. Jones finally said.

Paul didn't answer. It took a long time for the comment even to filter into his thoughts. Then Paul was even more distracted, trying to decide whether he could bring all this up to a teacher. And if he did, what questions would he ask?

That was when Mr. Jones saw the praying mantises. "Look!" he said excitedly to Paul. "They're mating. Let's see how good a lover he is."

The two snuck closer. They watched as the relatively smaller male mounted the larger female. The whole act took only a matter of moments. When it was over, the male dismounted and moved away.

"He must have been good," Mr. Jones commented wryly.

Paul thought for a few seconds. There must be a lot more to this sex thing than he thought. How could Mr. Jones tell anything about the praying mantis' mating technique from what they had just seen? He finally got up the nerve to ask.

"How could you tell he was good, Mr. Jones?"

"You see, Paul," the teacher explained. "There is a myth that the female praying mantis always kills her lover after sex. But that isn't true. If her lover mounts her very skillfully, she doesn't kill him. But if he is clumsy in his approach, she just turns her long neck around and bites his head off. Then the poor guy functions naturally long enough to impregnate her."

An image quickly floated through Paul's mind. He was thankful that this technique didn't apply to humans. What had happened in his parents' bedroom had seemed ugly enough.

"Does that myth apply to humans at all, Mr. Jones?" he asked.

"It certainly does, Paul," Mark Jones answered excitedly, and Paul knew right away that he wasn't going to have to ask any more questions. His teacher liked nothing more than an eager student.

"Take your right hand, extend it straight out in front of you and raise it in the air," he directed. Paul did as he was told.

"Now, suppose I were to ask you right now to raise your penis." Paul gulped and his face turned several shades of red, but Mr. Jones only smiled calmly. "Don't worry, Paul. It was only a hypothetical question." Paul relaxed just a little. "You see, sex is not controlled by the voluntary nervous system the way your arm is. It's controlled by the autonomic nervous system—like your heart is. Furthermore, it is controlled by that part of the autonomic nervous system that is called the 'relaxation response.' So, if sex is going to work, it's important that a person not feel pressured to perform. People can't will themselves to have sex. They have to get their heads out of the way and let their bodies respond."

"And, if a person was used to using alcohol or some other substance to relax and then stopped using that substance," Paul asked excitedly, "it could cause him problems sexually?" He was now fascinated by the discussion and momentarily forgot his self-consciousness.

"That is a very good question, Paul," Mr. Jones said with pride. "Yes, it certainly could cause him problems."

Paul was so impressed with his teacher's knowledge and the calm manner in which he discussed such a difficult subject that he just had to ask another question that had been bothering him.

"Mr. Jones, the word around school is that you're not married and that you don't date. How can you know all this if you don't apply it?"

Mr. Jones laughed. "Well, I've never been lucky enough to date a praying mantis, but I do know that this is what the whole thing is about, Paul: you can't make love with your head. That's the part the female bites off. You have got to make love with your heart."

Suddenly, Paul knew that if he could somehow tell his dad about the praying mantises it would make a difference. But how? He couldn't just walk up to his dad and say, "Listen Dad, I know you're having sexual problems and I can help."

Mark Jones stood up and yawned. "Most of the boats seem settled in for the night and the loons seem to be doing the same, Paul. I think I'll knock off. Do you want a ride home?"

"No thanks, Mr. Jones," Paul answered. "I think I'll stay here for a while and then run home. You know, me and Sally have been running every morning and I'm actually beginning to enjoy it. Of course, I'd never tell her that. She thinks I'm doing her this incredible favor and I want to be able to take advantage of that at some point."

The teacher laughed. "OK, Paul. Will you be by here tomorrow?"

"You bet!" Paul answered.

It was late afternoon, and Paul waited and listened to the loon's wail a few more times. To Paul, the beauty of that sound made taking all the ridicule worthwhile. Then he jogged home. On the way he thought some more about how he could share what he learned with his father. This was what he had come to like about running: it gave him time to think.

As he jogged, he developed a plan.

CHAPTER IX

When Paul arrived home, dinner was just about ready. Unlike the other night, everyone was at the table. Hank and Molly were busy arguing, but this time not with each other. They were trying to convince Sally that she should eat with the family now that the track season was over. She finally agreed, but Paul noticed she spent most of her time pushing the food around her plate. The others seemed preoccupied with their own plates, however, and the family ate in silence.

The Brandts had probably always been a family that concentrated more on eating than talking. During the years of Hank's drinking, everyone ate with one eye on the door, wondering when and in what condition he'd come home. But tonight it was not just the tension in his family that was obvious to Paul. It was the distance between each of them.

He waited until dinner was nearly finished. His mother and father were sipping their coffee and Ryan had just taken his last swallow of milk. "Mr. Jones taught me about sex today," Paul said matter-of-factly.

It was probably the absurdity of it that got to all of them. Here they were, in their deadliest, coldest silence, and timid Paul brings up the biggest taboo subject of all. Ryan sprayed his milk across the table. Molly spilled most of her coffee trying to calmly place the cup in her saucer. Sally started giggling uncontrollably, and Bobbie immediately focused all of her attention on the spills. She got up from the table and called Ryan a pig, then went to the kitchen sink for a rag and began furiously moving dishes and wiping up milk and coffee wherever she could find it. Perhaps the strangest reaction came from Hank. He raised his hand in the air to try to quiet the bedlam and with a smile that carried some relief he said to Paul, "What did he teach you?"

As soon as Paul started to talk, however, everyone else in the family started to talk at the same time. Hank again raised his hand, but this time lowered it with more authority. "Quiet!" he said calmly. "What's the matter with you people? Aren't we grown up enough to have a discussion on this subject without mass hysteria? Now, I want to hear what Paul has to say." The kitchen again grew quiet—not so much from tension now as from shock and amazement at both Paul and Hank.

Everyone's amazement grew as Paul made his presentation. To his recollection, Paul had never before had the attention of his entire family all at once, and to have that attention at the request of his father felt to him like making his debut on Broadway. He proceeded to tell them all about the praying mantises and how the male lives if he mounts his mate the right way. Paul thought at that point he caught his father glancing at his mother, but he wasn't sure.

Everyone howled with laughter when Paul said, "Then the poor guy functions naturally long enough to impregnate her."

Enjoying the laughter coming in his direction for a change, Paul quipped, "Well, you get the point." Next, Paul used Mark Jones's example about raising somebody's right arm and he used his father to demonstrate. When he then said to his father, "Now suppose I were to ask you to get an erection," bedlam returned. "Oh my God!" Sally shrieked.

Ryan was holding his sides and rocking back and forth, with short bursts of laughter erupting before he contained himself again. Molly simply sat with her mouth open and Bobbie started cleaning again. Hank was too shocked to establish order right away. So Paul said, "Relax guys! It's just a hypothetical question," and went straight into his discussion of the nervous system.

Paul left out the part about Mr. Jones and his dating life because he thought that was something his teacher had told him in confidence. He also knew that if Ryan and Sally heard that part of the story, it would be all over the school system by Monday morning. So he ended with, "And Mr. Jones says that's why you have to make love with your heart, rather than your head."

Sally finally got herself together enough to make a joke. "That was great, Paul," she said. "What will tomorrow's lecture be on—sex and the single mosquito?" Everyone laughed, but they applauded Paul at the same time.

Paul acknowledged the applause. "Thank you," he said. "Now may I be excused? I have to go to the bathroom." As he ran up the stairs, he heard them all laughing and commenting on what he had said.

When Paul reached the bathroom, he had a queasy feeling in his stomach. He realized that he was just excited . . . and proud. Pride was a new feeling for Paul. He decided that he liked it.

Paul spent most of the rest of the night in his room.

He had had all the interpersonal interaction he thought he could handle for one day. As he lay quietly in his bed, he heard someone enter the bathroom and then vomit. I guess I'm not the only one whose stomach is upset, he thought. A few moments later, Sally stuck her head in the door. "Going running in the morning, Paul? We've got a lot to talk about," she said with a devilish grin.

Paul had to work hard to get the pained "I hate running" expression on his face. "I guess so," he said, sounding burdened. "Hey, are you O.K.?" he asked.

"Sure," she replied with a surprised look on her face.

Next Bobbie looked in. "Is that really true about the praying mantis?" she asked.

"I guess so," he answered.

Bobbie looked a little confused herself and closed the door quickly.

Last came Ryan. He stuck his head in the door and in a deadly serious voice said, "Now suppose I ask you to have an erection?" Ryan didn't wait for a reply. Paul could hear peals of laughter as Ryan retreated down the hall.

Paul pretended to be asleep when Ryan came to bed so he could hear what was going on in his parents' room. Ryan was quickly in bed and the lights were off. The room was quiet and Paul listened intently.

Then from the dark corner over by the window came Ryan's voice. "Now suppose I ask you to have an erection?" The last part of the sentence was hard to understand because Ryan was laughing so hard. Paul felt on the floor for a shoe. He found one and threw it. It hit Ryan as Paul had hoped, but it only encouraged his brother all the more.

"Now suppose. . . ." More laughter.

Heck with it, Paul thought. It's up to them now. I've done what I can. Soon he heard his dad snoring. He thought about what Mr. Jones had said. "Knowing is not enough; you have to make love with your heart." Perhaps the heart takes its time, Paul thought as he drifted off to sleep.

After that night, the dinner table at the Brandt house seemed a lot less tense. There was a lot more laughing, and people began to bring up all kinds of issues and feelings. One night Molly commented on the change.

"Heck, Mom," Ryan said. "After Paul's lecture on sex, what could anyone else do or say that would shock this family?" They all laughed, including Paul.

CHAPTER X

In spite of Paul's new-found interpersonal success, he still liked his solitude. It was more than the loons and nesting site that kept Paul on the other side of the lake and away from the public beach that summer. Paul enjoyed being alone. Though the bottom of the lake on that side was mucky and brown, Paul still preferred to swim there by himself, away from the clean and sandy but crowded public beach. He didn't like sunning himself anyway, and his thin, pre-pubescent body was certainly nothing to show off. Besides, the swampy part of the lake provided many more bugs, frogs and pollywogs to study.

Mark Jones kept a dinghy with a small outboard motor on it near the nesting site. He didn't mind if Paul took it out now and then. The two loners were becoming good friends. In spite of the fact that the loons stayed and the female laid two eggs this time, the other Loonies had lost interest, so Paul was often at the site alone.

So Paul was surprised when Zack Pierce showed up one afternoon.

It seemed to Paul that with each passing day Zack became more handsome. His now dark brown body stood in stark contrast to his blond hair bleached lighter by the sun. His light blue eyes seemed to gaze from deep behind his tanned face. But it was the person behind the face that was most attractive to Paul. It's been said that God gives alcoholism to those he wants to draw closer to, and it was easy to see why God would want to be closer to Zack. He was kind and gentle and wasn't afraid to show it, even when he was surrounded by his athlete friends. He was wise for a young person, and yet humble. Zack would talk to anyone without putting on an air of being better than his listener.

Zack had grown uncomfortable with the drinking and smoking going on at Roper's, so he had decided to take a walk and check out Paul and the loons. He had taken the path that led through the woods around the lake to the loon nesting site.

Sitting quietly underneath a shade tree, Paul was watching a bass jump for mayflies. He was startled when Zack walked up behind him. "Hi!" Zack said rather softly, but loud enough to make Paul jump higher than the bass.

"Sorry, Paul, I didn't mean to startle you," Zack apologized.

"I thought your specialty was scaring loons," Paul said, embarrassed by his reaction.

"Paul, I wasn't even here that day," Zack said evenly. "And I'm sorry it happened. I like listening to the birds at night, too."

Paul's mood changed when he heard Zack was also an admirer of the loons. "I can never decide if I like the yodel or the wail the best," Paul said enthusiastically.

"What's the difference?" Zack asked.

"The wail is shorter, and it's for calling its mate. The yodel is a long series of calls, and it's used when the loon's territory is invaded," Paul answered.

"How'd you get here, anyway?" Paul asked suddenly, realizing Zack didn't totally share his passion for loons.

"I was just walking around the lake, " Zack said.

"What, are you bored with drinking and smoking at Roper's?" Paul said sarcastically.

"Drinking? Smoking?" Zack said, trying to looked shocked.

"You know, Zack, your friends may consider me a geek, but I'm not stupid," Paul countered.

"Well, if you're so smart you ought to know I'm recovering and don't do that stuff anymore," Zack replied strongly.

"Oh, yeah, I forgot," said Paul, apologetically. "Sorry."

"It's O.K.," Zack said. "In a way, I'm glad people forget. I guess that means you don't see me as some sort of freak."

"Are you kidding?" Paul exclaimed. "You're the only one of my brother's friends that I like, and that's because you don't treat me like I'm a freak."

"Thanks, Paul. You're a good kid and I like you, too," Zack answered sincerely.

"Now that that's out of the way, how are you doing with girls this summer?" Paul asked, trying to change the subject and sound like one of the guys in the locker room.

"Hold on there, young one. Just because I like you doesn't mean I'm ready to share my life history with you," Zack said somewhat playfully.

"I'm sorry," Paul responded. "It's just that Mr. Jones and I were talking a few days ago about . . ."

"Oh, yeah, Ryan told me about the famous praying mantis dinner conversation," Zack said with a laugh. "Well, I date a little bit, but my sponsor suggested I make recovery my number one priority for a while longer. So I don't have a lot of experiences

I can share with you. No girl has bit my head off yet, if that's what you're wondering."

The two boys laughed. Then they sat for a long time watching the fish and the birds. It was getting later in the afternoon and the activity on the lake was beginning to die down.

"I think I'll swim back to Roper's now," Zack said.

Paul looked at him in disbelief. "You sure you weren't smoking some of that weed before you left?" he protested. "That swim across to Roper's is at least a mile, and those people out there on those power boats aren't that observant—even when they're sober.

"We swim farther than that in practice, Paul, and the boats aren't allowed to come closer than 100 feet to the shore," Zack replied as he started to wade into the water.

"Well, how about if I ride alongside you in the dinghy?" Paul offered.

"No, that's O.K.," Zack assured Paul. "You've got the loons to protect and, besides, I've done this hundreds of times."

With powerful strokes, Zack was well on his way back to Roper's within minutes. Paul watched him swim. Zack had always been friendly to him. Maybe it was his good looks and athletic ability that gave

Zack the confidence he needed to be friendly with someone like Paul who wasn't "cool." Paul marvelled at the speed with which he moved through the water. His admiration turned to horror, however, when he saw Roper's boat, along with the "tubers" he was pulling, heading at full speed in Zack's direction.

Tubing is like water-skiing, except the "tubers" are pulled by ropes behind a powerboat on large inner tubes, usually truck or tractor tubes. It isn't as challenging as water skiing, because it is easier to stay on. Easier, that is, unless whoever is driving the boat goes very fast and makes sharp turns, whipping the tubes with centrifugal force out over the wake of the boat. Tubing is probably dangerous under the best of conditions, but this was near dusk and these kids had obviously been drinking.

Roper delighted in his ability to lose anyone off a tube within a few minutes and enjoyed watching their bodies turn over several times on top of the water before sinking. At the moment, Ryan and Steve were on the tubes, with Roper driving. Mike, another friend, was supposed to be watching the tubers in case one fell, while the driver watched for other boats. Both Mike and Roper, however, were watching the boys being whipped around turn after turn. As the boat gradually headed in Zack's direction, Paul decided to follow Zack in the dinghy and ride next to him in spite of Zack's earlier refusal.

The small motor on the dinghy propelled Paul slowly through the water. He had a sick feeling inside. He tried logically to convince himself that the chances of the swimmer and the boat being at the same place at the same time were remote, but his feeling of doom didn't subside. Paul wished that Zack would swim slower or that the dinghy would move faster or that Roper would turn around and look where he was going. Paul was gaining on Zack, but not as rapidly as Roper was.

Even with the turns and zig-zags Roper made as he tried his best to get Ryan and Steve off the tubes, the powerful boat moved steadily in Zack's direction. Paul tried waving his arms, to no avail. Even if Roper were looking at him, which he wasn't, he would have probably thought Paul was trying to wave him away from the nesting site. In the water, Zack wasn't wearing goggles and couldn't possibly see the boat coming towards him.

The final moments all seemed to happen in slow motion to Paul: the speedboat full of partying and ignorant bliss; Zack's relaxed, powerful, confident strokes; and Paul's panic and screams, drowned by the motors. The collision seemed imminent. Paul hoped that Zack would hear Roper's boat coming close and dive under the water. Just as the boat was about to hit him, Zack did look up and dive, but Paul wasn't sure that Zack had time to avoid the prop. Roper's boat sped blissfully past and away from Zack, unaware of the possible collision. Paul, his heart in his throat, begged his tiny engine to speed up. He kept hoping to see Zack's head bob out of the water any second. Instead, he saw a crimson slick on the water, which confirmed his worst fears.

Just as Paul arrived at the spot, Zack's pale face emerged from the pool of reddening water. Paul struggled to pull the boy into the dinghy, and he nearly passed out when he saw Zack's ankle and foot. Zack seemed to be in shock, but Paul kept talking to him as he wrapped his tee shirt around the wound.

On the next turn of Roper's boat, Ryan saw Paul pulling Zack into the dinghy. He tried to wave to get Roper's and Mike's attention, but as soon as he did he flew from the tube. The two laughed and circled to pick him up.

"I knew I'd get you off. You owe me five bucks," Roper shouted with pride in his voice.

Ryan screamed to Roper, "Zack's hurt! Get us in the boat." Once Ryan and Steve were back in the boat, Roper turned around and sped up beside Paul.

"Killing loons wasn't enough for you?" Paul cried as the boat came within shouting distance. When the older boys saw Zack's injuries, they transferred him into Roper's boat and quickly took off, leaving Paul behind in the dinghy, totally ignored.

The teenagers were terrified. Would their friend be all right? And what were they going to tell the authorities about how the accident happened? While driving Zack to the hospital, they agreed on a story. Roper suggested they say they were going slowly and the boat was riding high in the front, so they didn't see Zack. They all also agreed to insist that Zack had wandered too far out from shore.

Zack, who was in great pain and kept going in and out of consciousness, agreed to the story, as long as Roper's insurance would cover all the damages. The boys all promised they would say nothing about drinking or drugging and, if asked, would deny it.

"What about Paul?" Roper asked. "Will he go along with the story? Do you think he knows we were drinking?"

"I don't know," Ryan said. "He's pretty mad at us about the loon thing. I don't think I can convince him to keep quiet about this."

"I'll talk to Paul," Roper said, sounding mean.

"Don't hurt him," Ryan growled.

"Hey, do you want your old man to find out you were drinking?" Roper yelled. "I'm trying to save your butt." Ryan was silent.

As soon as Roper could slip out of the hospital emergency room without being noticed, he left. On the way out, he saw Paul, who was just arriving on his bike from the lake.

"Hey, Paul! Wait up," Roper called.

Against his better judgment, Paul waited. "What do *you* want?" he asked in the toughest tone he could muster.

"I just want to say thanks," Roper said, sounding kind. "You really saved my hide."

"I didn't do it for you," Paul asserted in disgust.

"Of course not," said Roper. "You did it to save Zack. You're a hero. I'll make sure that everyone knows about it," Roper answered, remaining calm.

Paul caught on to the kindness act, which had fooled him at first. "Oh, I get it," he said. "I'm a hero and you're nice to me in return for just a few modifications on the facts, right?" Paul said, his voice rising in anger. "Forget it, Roper, nothing will please me more than getting you and your buddies in trouble. Maybe your parents will even take away your precious boat."

Roper grabbed Paul by the nape of the neck and dragged him behind the building. "You want to make another tombstone for those two new eggs?" Roper threatened. "And maybe have one made for yourself?"

Few people could intimidate as well as Roper, and Paul was genuinely scared. Roper must have discovered the grave the Loonies had made for the first egg. Several thoughts raced through Paul's mind. Had the boys truly missed seeing Zack merely because they were caught up in having a good time, or was it because alcohol and marijuana had made them oblivious? Paul didn't mind covering for kids just having fun, but what was the difference between a speedboat on a lake and a car on the highway? Drunk drivers have no business in either place. But what about the loons? They were innocent victims too. Paul couldn't bear to see two more babies die. The combination of fear of Roper and compassion for the loons made his decision for him.

"I'll go along with your lies," Paul said, trying not to sound scared. "But you leave the loons alone!"

A sneer came over Roper's face. "I'll treat them like family," he said sarcastically.

CHAPTER XI

This was to be a family day for the Brandts. First, most of them were going to see Sally run in a race with her summer park district team. Then, it would be on to Bobbie's graduation ceremonies in the evening. Paul was leaving his room when he noticed Sally pacing back and forth in hers.

"Nervous?" he asked as he stepped inside.

"Yeah," she said, continuing to pace. "And Dad made me eat a sandwich, saying I couldn't run on an empty stomach." She rolled her eyes and continued. "I hate running on a full stomach." She looked at her profile in the mirror. She seemed disgusted.

"Well, one sandwich won't hurt," Paul reasoned. "By the time your race comes up you'll probably be hungry rather than full. Those meets take forever, and you're in one of the last events. Besides, there's no more time to worry. We have to go."

"You go ahead," Sally said with a smile. "I have to go to the bathroom one more time. Nerves, you know." She patted him on the back as they walked from her bedroom, her mood seemingly improved.

By the time Sally ran to the car where Paul, Ryan and her mother and father were waiting, she seemed exhilarated. It was obvious that cares and worries wouldn't be slowing her down today.

Paul was right when he anticipated the meet being long, but it was worth the wait to see Sally run. As she lined up for the mile race, her body didn't stand out; she was just as thin as the other girls. When the gun sounded, she immediately grabbed the lead. As she pulled away, her strides seemed effortless and natural. By the end of the race, she led by several yards. She crossed the finish line looking as though she had just stepped off a bus. The Brandts all jumped and cheered. Sally looked up at the stands with an embarrassed grin and shook her head, but her pride showed through.

That night at Bobbie's graduation from high school, the family was all there to watch her. Even Scott, who had become more and more withdrawn from the family since the intervention, came home from college for the event. The ceremony seemed long and boring to Paul, and he couldn't wait to get out. On the ride home, Bobbie was crying softly in the back seat and Ryan was teasing her.

"Boy, you can bet I won't cry when I graduate!" he promised.

"You mean *if* you graduate, don't you son?" Hank quipped.

"Now, can't we be nice to each other on this special night?" Molly said. "We're very proud of you, Bobbie. You did a great job in high school."

"Thanks, Mom," Bobbie said. "I just wish I had started to get involved socially sooner than I did. I feel like I just met most of my friends in the last year, and now we'll all be separating and going to different schools."

Before the intervention with Hank, Bobbie had been so involved in keeping peace in the family that she really hadn't taken time for friends. But since that time, she had started dating a boy named Tom, and they both hung around with the same group friends. Tom was going to be attending the same college as Scott. In fact, he would be leaving for summer school the following week. His grades in high school had not been the best, and he needed the summer courses to prove his ability to the college.

Bobbie, on the other hand, although she had been the top student in her class, was planning to attend the local community college for at least one year. Molly and Hank had asked her to do that until Scott finished college the following year. They said the reason was financial, but Paul thought it was really because Bobbie helped keep the family stable and they were afraid of losing her presence too soon. He also believed Bobbie wanted to stay at home because she still felt so responsible for the family. But Paul kept all these opinions to himself.

"You know," Hank said later that night as they all sat around the kitchen table eating the cake Molly had made for Bobbie. "A lot has happened in the last year that we have to be thankful for. I got sober, Paul is a hero, Bobbie graduated, Sally's a track star, Scott continues to excel in class and on the football field, Molly was named music director at church, and Ryan got his driver's license and a part-time job. I think it's time that we had a big Brandt family party, like we used to have."

"Oh, Hank. Do you think we're ready for something like that?" Molly asked nervously.

"Molly, it's been a year. We can't hide from alcohol forever. I know I can't drink, but I don't have to avoid fun, too, do I?"

The children all seconded Hank's idea. Scott

promised to come home again for the party. Molly finally relented.

Over the next few days, however, Molly continued to argue with Hank about serving alcohol at the party. Hank insisted it would not bother him and that he would feel funny not having anything to offer his friends. Realizing it was useless to pursue the point, Molly gave in. But as the day of the party grew closer, all of the old tension began to surface between them. Paul could tell that just having alcohol in the house again made Molly uncomfortable.

The party took place on the following weekend. Pastor Brooks came, and having him there was a great comfort to Molly. Hank's brother, Ken, and his wife, Martha, were also there, as were most of the men who worked with Ken and Hank.

Scott was there, too, with a girlfriend. He seemed to have a cold, because his nose was running constantly. He appeared uncomfortable around the other people, and every once in a while he would leave and take a walk. After one of these walks, Paul thought he noticed that Scott and his girlfriend were fighting. Shortly after that, Scott said he wasn't feeling well, and they left.

Bobbie had invited almost her entire high school class, and most of them came. It was obvious she was really enjoying herself, and at one point she went up to her father and gave him a big hug. "Thanks, Daddy! I know you did this for me." She was crying again, with joy. Hank didn't say anything. He just shook his head, because he knew he would be crying, too, if he tried to talk.

The party was a wonderful mixture of young and old. Hank was the perfect host, not pushing alcohol but offering it as an option when people asked for a drink. He also made sure none of Bobbie's or Ryan's friends drank. Paul could see that Molly tried very hard not to watch her husband when he made drinks next to her in the kitchen while she was fixing food. She never mentioned anything to him about the alcohol.

Towards the end of the party, she even let Hank pour her a glass of wine.

As the last people left the party and the family was all helping with the cleanup, everyone seemed relieved—not only because the planning and effort of putting together a large event were over, but also because the party itself had gone well, without any incidents or disagreements. Even cleaning up together was fun. Sally made jokes and Ryan teased Bobbie unmercifully about Tom. They all fell into bed that night, tired from the events of the day.

Everyone, that is, except Paul. Midway through the party, he had walked past the pantry to find his father furtively sipping a drink. It was an alcoholic drink, Paul instinctively knew. In shock, he walked out of the kitchen without Hank noticing him. For the rest of the evening, however, Paul had kept a watchful eye on his dad. As near as he could tell, it was Hank's only slip.

Like everything else Paul was carrying on his frail little shoulders, this was a heavy burden. He slept little that night.

CHAPTER XII

When they first started, running had been drudgery to both Sally and Paul. Sally did it only to lose weight and to have an excuse to be out of the house, and Paul did it only as a favor to Sally.

"You know," Sally said to Paul on one of the first mornings of summer vacation, "I have never been very active, and my weight made it difficult for me to feel good doing physical things. When track season started, I had trouble running around the track once without stopping to rest. I wanted to be able to run with the other kids, so I pushed myself hard and stayed late to run extra laps. By the end of the season, I could run more than a mile and my times were dropping and I was winning races. Now I'm really getting to the point that I enjoy running. I can't wait for next fall's cross country season. "

The two of them looked like a precision drill team as they moved down the road. Their feet landed at the same time, their strides were equal, even their arms moved in unison.

"You don't even have to run with me anymore, Paul," she announced. "I know I'll keep going on my own."

"I've been playing with you, Sal," Paul confessed. "I enjoy running now, too."

"I thought you did," she said with a smile. "Besides, you're getting good at it. You should go out for cross country in the fall, too."

"No. I want it to be something I do just for myself," Paul said.

"You know, I've lived with you all my life and I still don't understand you," Sally said. "Why don't you want to show off something you're good at?"

"It's not that I don't want to show off," Paul countered. "It's just that if I do it as a sport I'll have coaches telling me when I have to run and how far, and I'm afraid they'll ruin it for me."

"That makes some sense," Sally said with a laugh. "But you're still weird."

Paul lightly punched her on the arm. They ran for a while in silence.

"Since you're being so free with the compliments,"

Paul said with a smile, "I can tell that you really have lost weight. How much have you lost since we started running?"

"I don't know," Sally said quickly, "I'm afraid to step on the scale because I'm still so fat."

Paul looked at her with curiosity. "I don't think you're fat at all any more," he said. "As a matter of fact, you need to go back to eating regularly. You probably will keep losing weight just because you run so much."

"Well, maybe you're right," Sally replied, "but don't start bugging me like Mom and Dad, O.K.?"

"O.K.," Paul promised.

At the beginning of summer, they had made an agreement to get up and run early every morning. That way, they could run when it was cool. The two youngsters had reached, by now, the point where they felt they could run forever. They would leave the house just after sunrise and run toward the lake, where they would watch the mist rising off the water as they ran in the coolness among the trees. Paul would stop and check on the loons.

After running for several minutes without stopping, they felt as if their legs were no longer attached to their bodies. They moved effortlessly, and their minds were free to wander. Brother and sister could think or talk about things or just watch the world go by as it gradually woke from its slumber. Occasionally, on warmer mornings, they'd wear swimming suits under their shorts and take a dip in the lake before running back home.

This particular morning, Paul watched as Sally poured herself some cereal. He was pleased to see her eat a few bites, but then she poured most of it down the sink. She spread bread crumbs on a plate to make it look as if she had eaten more than she really had. Sally had really become an expert at moving food around so it appeared as if she had eaten.

Hank and Molly walked in just as Sally was leaving the kitchen. She greeted them cheerfully, giving each a kiss on the cheek.

"Oh, are we in one of our friendly moods today?" her mother asked.

"Aren't I always?" Sally answered, stopping dead in her tracks as if she had just been caught stealing from the cookie jar.

"No, you're not," Hank said, chiming in on the conversation. "You know, Sally, I never thought I of all people would say this to one of my kids, but don't you think you're overdoing this exercise bit a little?"

"You're right, Dad; this is a shock," Sally said, trying to maintain a playful air. "You've always pushed us kids to be in sports and do our best. You've always seemed disappointed that no one has followed in Scott's jock footsteps."

"I know," Hank replied slowly, "but I think you're losing too much weight. And you seem so tired and moody."

"All that didn't seem to bother you when I was coming in first at the meets you came to this spring," Sally snapped, finally raising her voice.

Hank sighed in desperation. "I'm proud of what you've accomplished, Sally, but your health is more important to me than all your victories combined," he said, trying to remain calm.

"I wonder if you'd say that if I were a boy?" Sally yelled. "Paul runs every day and you don't stop him."

"Paul runs once in the morning and he's not losing weight. Plus, he eats a lot more than you do," Molly retorted.

"I don't understand," Sally screamed. "When I finally do something I think will please you, you get mad at me for doing it. I just can't win in this family."

"O.K., I've had it," Hank shouted back. "I don't want you running any more before dinner, when you will sit down with the family and eat. Molly, you sit down with her now and make sure she eats a decent breakfast," Hank said as he stormed out of the house.

"I ate already," Sally objected, calling after him.

"I know how you ate," her father yelled back.

Sally sat down at the table and slowly ate cereal and a piece of toast. Paul left the kitchen as quickly and as quietly as he could, but Molly sat with her daughter long after she had finished her own breakfast.

"What's wrong with you, Sally?" Molly finally asked. "You used to be so cheerful and ready with a joke, but now you seem almost depressed much of the time.

"Running raises your sugar level and you don't feel hungry right afterwards, Mom," Sally explained. "If I weren't forced to sit here now after coming home from running I would eat better later and I wouldn't be so crabby."

"O.K.," Molly said logically. "Then maybe you'll be hungry by dinner if you don't run any more today."

Sally left the table in tears and went to her room. Paul heard her and went to see how she was doing. When he poked his head into the room, Sally was looking at herself in the mirror. "I dread the thought of having to eat dinner, especially if I didn't earn it with a run," she told Paul.

"Sally, you're not fat any more," Paul tried to reason. "With all the exercise you're getting, you don't have to worry about your weight."

Her mood seemed to lighten. "I guess you're right," she said as she moved past him toward the door. "Now if you'll excuse me, I have to go to the bathroom."

Paul knew his sister well, and it seemed to him that recently he could change her mind with only a few words. Maybe he wasn't changing her mind at all. After each discussion, she seemed to cheer up as she headed for the bathroom.

This time Paul listened closely and heard her throw up.

Paul waited outside the bathroom door. When Sally opened the door and saw Paul there, she knew she had been heard. "Don't you dare say a word," she snarled at Paul.

Another secret, Paul thought.

After that, Paul and Sally ran separately.

CHAPTER XIII

Pastor Brooks had called Molly several times during the week before reaching her. "Where have you been?" he asked, sounding slightly perturbed.

"Oh, grocery shopping, clothes shopping, running kids around—you know how it is."

"Yes, I guess I do," he said vaguely. "Listen, I'd like you to do me a favor, Molly. I'd like you to bring your whole family to church this weekend. Do you think they would come?"

"I'm sure they'd come. What's the occasion?" she asked suspiciously.

There was a long pause at the other end of the line. "I'd rather just explain it to you at church, if that's all right," he said.

"Sure," Molly replied. She hung up the phone.

What was that all about, she wondered.

Molly told the family that night about Pastor Brooks's request, and they all agreed to go to the first service the next Sunday.

When they arrived at the church, Molly started to open the organ and found a note addressed to her on the music stand. She opened it quickly, thinking it had something to do with the music the pastor wanted her to play that day. She froze as she read the short note.

"Molly, I will be announcing today that I'm being transferred. I wanted you to know first." It was signed "Love, John Brooks."

Molly played mechanically through the early parts of the service, waiting for the sermon to confirm this harsh reality. It appeared to Molly that Pastor Brooks's eyes were already watering as he approached the pulpit. As intellectual as ever, he began with a quotation.

"I think it was the famous psychoanalyst Carl Gustav Jung who said 'Life itself can be seen as a slow progressive disease from which there is a poor prognosis for recovery.' Before I came to this parish I felt that, in many ways, this statement summed up my philosophy of life."

The congregation stirred visibly. This was not going to be a normal homily.

"I was a part of the living dead until all of you

came into my life," he continued. "I used to think I knew life because I was such a good observer. You have all taught me, however, to be a participant, and now I see things very differently. Joshua Krueger was an inspiration to me—as I know he was to many of you. His love of music still rings through this parish each Sunday morning. Since his death, all of you have continued to nurture me and give me life. I feel I've grown up in your loving arms. You have been the compassionate, forgiving family that has helped me to mature, personally and professionally, over the last year."

The stirring had been replaced by absolute silence. Pastor Brooks continued. "One of the things that has helped me to grow has been learning about the philosophies of the various 12-step recovery programs that some of you, my dear friends, are involved in and have shared with me. I've learned much from you about recovery and relapse."

Molly shot a quick glance at Hank, but his eyes were on the floor.

"Recovery is an ongoing, living growth process, and relapse is the absence of recovery," the pastor went on. "There is no such thing as being cured. To avoid relapse, one must actively pursue recovery. Now, this is where my quote from Jung ties in. You see, it's not just you alcoholic or drug addicted families out there that must embrace recovery. It's all of us. We are either in the process of getting better as a people, or we're getting worse. We all need to pursue recovery if we want to avoid relapse. We are either growing and embracing life or we are deteriorating and submitting to death."

There was a definite murmuring from the congregation now. They weren't sure they liked what they were going to hear.

"The last years have been the happiest time of my life," Pastor Brooks proclaimed in a strong voice. "I could have chosen to stay here in the security of this parish family. But, I've decided that I, too, have to continue changing and that I, too, have to share with others what I've learned. I've been offered a chance to teach at the seminary. I believe that now I have something to share with prospective clergy that might help them begin 'recovering' earlier than I did. So it is time for me to say thank you and good-bye to you, my family that has nursed me into life. I can say with all sincerity that I love you and I'll miss you. May we all continue to move toward life!"

John Brooks paused to wipe away his tears. Many in the congregation did the same.

"Now, let me hear those wonderful voices that will continue to be a source of inspiration to me for my entire life!" Pastor Brooks concluded. He turned to Molly to signal her to begin the hymn and gave her the kindest smile she could remember since Josh Krueger did the same thing over a year before.

Molly cried on and off through the rest of the service. They weren't exactly tears of sadness. She felt happy for her friend, although she knew she would miss him fiercely. On the church steps afterwards, she hugged Pastor Brooks. There was little need for words between them. Then the whole family said good-bye. Though the minister had been closest to Molly, he had been a part of all of their lives. When he got to Paul, he said, "I think that, out of your whole family, I identify most with you, Paul. Next to your mother, I will miss you most of all."

Somehow, Paul realized that from Pastor Brooks's sermon he had the theme for another dinner lecture.

CHAPTER XIV

The injury to Zack Pierce was not as serious as the doctors first thought, but it was still a welcome sight when Paul saw him through the binoculars walking toward the loon site. It was an exciting day for Paul, because the two baby loons had just hatched. After their parents had cleaned them up, they looked like two little balls of fluff. To Paul, they were the cutest things he had ever laid eyes on.

"Next to those two loon babies, seeing you walking normally is the best thing I've seen in a long time," Paul said to Zack as he arrived at the site.

"You mean they've hatched?" Zack asked, genuinely excited. "Can I see?" He grabbed the binoculars from Paul and put them up to his eyes. The cord, however, was still around Paul's neck. Zack didn't seem to notice Paul's discomfort as he peered at the two babies.

"Wow, they're brown!" Zack exclaimed. "I never expected them to be brown."

Paul tapped the taller boy on the shoulder, but Zack kept looking and talking. "Zack," Paul finally said. "The cord!"

Zack finally put down the binoculars and Paul took a deep breath. Zack looked down at the cord attached to the binoculars, and then at Paul's face as it gradually changed from purple to pink. First he started to laugh, and then he apologized. "Oh, Paul, I'm sorry," he said, still laughing a little. "Here you save my life, and this is how I treat you."

"Well, I don't think I saved your life. You only ended up with some stitches. Still, I do wish you wouldn't hang me with my own binoculars," Paul stammered.

"Paul," Zack said in a much more agitated voice. "You did save my life. True, I just had some stitches, but there were a lot of stitches. And when you pulled me out of that water I was in shock. I would have drowned. Paul, those others would never have noticed me if you hadn't been there. So don't minimize what you did. You're the reason I'm alive today and I'm here right now to thank you for that." Zack put his arm around Paul. "Thank you."

Paul rarely looked people in the eye, but he looked right at Zack and said, "You're welcome."

Then after a pause, Paul asked, "But how come you sound mad at me?"

"I'm not mad at you for saving my life, Paul. I'm mad at you for not giving yourself the credit you deserve," Zack said in a calmer tone. "But I mean it. Thank you."

Paul waved his hand and smiled. "It was nothing."

Zack put his fist to Paul's chin, but he was smiling. "Could I look at the babies again?" he asked. "This time I'll do it without the cord wrapped around your neck."

"Sure," Paul said, carefully removing the cord and handing him the binoculars.

As he looked at the babies, Zack's expression changed from excited to serious. "What's the matter?" Paul asked.

"There's another reason I came here, Paul, and it's not anywhere near as pleasant," Zack said in a somber tone.

"What's the matter?" Paul asked.

"I have remembered what actually happened the day you saved me, and I've decided to tell people about it. I have to tell my parents and your parents, for instance, and if I do that I know they'll tell Roper's parents."

Paul was terrified of the implications of Zack's announcement. "But if Roper gets in trouble, even if I'm not the one who told, he'll kill these babies for sure, just for spite," Paul blurted out. "Is your honesty worth those babies dying?"

"I know," Zack replied gently. "Ryan told me that Roper threatened you with killing the loons if you talked. That's why I got sad looking at them just now," Zack said.

"Then why would you tell, knowing that would happen?" Paul asked, wishing the tears weren't welling up in his eyes.

"Paul, this life that you saved won't be worth much to me if I go back to drinking and using drugs, and right now the only way that I can see to avoid that is to follow my 12-step program. The cornerstone to that program is honesty. If I don't tell what truly happened that day I will not only be dishonest, I will be enabling those guys to keep doing the kinds of things they are doing."

Just then, Roper's boat zoomed by in the middle of the lake.

"I know that he's out there right now and that he's been drinking. If I keep quiet, I may save the loons but people may die. I can't live with that responsibility and stay sober. I'm truly sorry, Paul, but I have to tell. And if it means my camping out here the rest of the summer to try to save these little birds, I'll do it. But I've got to tell."

"It doesn't matter if you camp out here. We're no match for Roper's boat," Paul said, the tears now streaming down his face.

"Maybe if Roper's parents find out what happened, they'll take his boat away," Zack countered.

"Yeah," Paul said, "and then he'll really be mad."

"There's an expression in the program, 'first things first,' " said Zack. "I've got to tell the truth first, and then I'll do what I can to help out with Roper. Do you understand, Paul?"

Paul again looked in Zack's eyes. He could see that Zack really was concerned about what Paul thought. "I understand," Paul said simply.

Then Paul had an idea. It was so perfect that he got very excited.

"Zack, since you want to tell my parents, how about if we do it together?" he suggested.

"Sure, but why?" Zack asked, curious at what his little friend was cooking up.

"Well, if Ryan's going to get confronted about the accident, then there are a few other things that ought to be mentioned. Ryan shouldn't be the only one in the family that gets heat for covering things up. Your being there would give me the courage to do some confronting of my own. And besides, some honesty might help my recovery, too," Paul said with a faraway look.

Zack looked at Paul strangely, but he quickly agreed. The two of them planned how they would do it. They finally decided to write letters, like people do during formal interventions. They felt that way they'd have a better chance of getting out exactly what they wanted to say, and the family would be more likely to hear them all the way through.

Paul and Zack each wrote his letter that night, and they met at the loon site the next day to review them with one another. Zack was a frequent dinner guest at the Brandt's anyway, so it was easy to arrange to have him over for dinner that night. As they prepared, Paul was happy to observe he wasn't the only one who was nervous.

CHAPTER XV

Paul and Zack were quiet at the Brandt dinner table that night, but no one seemed to notice. There was plenty of talking and everyone seemed relaxed. One of the reasons that Paul hated doing this confronting was that the people in his family were just getting comfortable with each other again. Everyone was just finishing up dinner when Zack and Paul pulled out their letters.

"We have a few things to say to all of you. Will you hear us out?" Zack asked calmly.

The room suddenly got very quiet. "Of course we'll listen," Hank said. They had all been through Hank's intervention and guessed that something serious was happening.

Zack went first.

Dear Ryan,

You have been my best friend since grade school. I truly value our friendship and the thought of losing it scares me to death, but we have little if we don't have honesty within that friendship. I can no longer live with continuing a lie about what truly happened the day I was hurt and what continues happening since then. I am afraid when you and Roper and your other friends drink and smoke and then go boating and skiing with his boat. I was not seriously hurt, but someone else—possibly you—may be someday, and I couldn't live with myself if I stood by and let that happen.

I care about you, Ryan, and that's why I'm saying this now. I don't want to get you in trouble, but I want what is going on to stop. I'm saying this in front of your parents because I don't believe either you or I can stop it on our own.

Love,
Zack

Ryan immediately looked at his father with fear in his eyes. He could see the anger building in Hank's face.

Before either of them had a chance to speak,

however, Zack spoke up again. "Paul has a few things he'd like to say before you react to this," he said. "Since without him I don't believe I would be alive today, I wish you'd listen to him." The room again got very quiet.

Paul had heard little of what Zack said. He had read a book recently called *Tales of the Loon*. It said that in Native American mythology warriors would go to the loon when they needed strength. They would hang on to the loon's wings as the loon dove deep into the water.

As he waited for Zack to finish, Paul too went to his brother, the loon, for strength. He could feel himself diving with the bird, and he hoped that when they reached the surface he would be strong enough to do what he had to do.

He heard Zack finishing just as he felt himself break out of the water. He started his own letter.

Dear Family,

A couple of weeks ago, we all went to church and heard Pastor Brooks talk about recovery and relapse. I'd like to start by saying I'm happy for the recovery of this family, but I'm also aware of all the ways we are relapsing, and I don't think we're being honest about those things. Zack says that honesty is the

> cornerstone to recovery. So I've decided that it's time I got honest.
>
> Dad, I'm proud of the effort you have been putting into your recovery. That is why when I saw you take a sip of alcohol at the party we had recently, it scared me. . . .

"I knew we shouldn't have had alcohol," Molly shouted. Hank looked confused, angry and embarrassed all at the same time.

"Mrs. Brandt," Zack interrupted. "Paul isn't finished and you promised you'd hear us out."

Molly became silent.

One by one, Paul named each of the family's secrets:

> Sally, I love you more than as a sister. You've been my best friend since you were born. I hate the distance that has come between us. But I can't sit by and watch you starve yourself. You throw up when Dad makes you eat, and you don't have a big meal at lunch like you say you do.
>
> We all know Scott is using cocaine, and, Bobbie, you spend time with him every weekend now and haven't said a thing about it. Besides, you should be going away to college

yourself but you won't because you don't think we can get along without you.

Mom is the only one of us that goes to Al-Anon meetings, even though we should all be going. And Mom, maybe we would go if you would act like they are doing you any good. But after a year, you're still trying to control Dad's drinking.

I love you all, but we all have to get more help.

Love,
Paul

The room was absolutely still as Paul finished his letter and then dove for the second time with the loon. Suddenly, everyone wanted to talk. Hank got his out first.

"I just took one sip to see if I could," he protested. "It's not like I relapsed."

"I told you we shouldn't have had booze in the house!" Molly screamed again.

Zack intervened. "You're right, Mr. Brandt. That wasn't the relapse." For the first time anyone in the family could remember, Zack sounded aggravated with them. "The relapse started long before that. It probably started with your paying less attention at meetings, then attending fewer meetings. It started with your listening less and talking less with your sponsor. It started when you began feeling angry, lonely, and even depressed without doing anything about it.

Hank started to react, but Zack continued. "And it didn't just start with you. It's not only your relapse, it's the whole family's relapse."

"And now, I'll say something else I probably shouldn't say," Zack concluded. "I've been a part of this family since I was little. I love every one of you. Each of you is a delightful person with special talents. What is so very sad is that not one of you believes in yourself or in each other. Now, you can let what Paul and I just shared destroy you or help you recover."

Zack's speech seemed to change the tone of the entire gathering. For the first time since the intervention, Hank started to cry. He didn't sob, but tears ran down his face as he turned to Molly. Hank's mere look could make anyone in the family feel small as an ant or tall as a building, but nothing had more power than his tears. Molly grabbed his hands.

"Molly, this isn't what we want," he said. "I feel like I'm back on the bottom again and I need your help to put the pieces back together. I need to know you still love me. In time, I hope you'll trust me again, too, but you have to let me make alcohol my problem."

"Why does it always take a crisis?" Molly cried

softly. "I'm sorry I've been so caught up in alcohol, Hank. I've been focused on it and oblivious to you, as strange as that may sound. You need to know that I'm committed to you and our family and that I do love you. It's time for me to focus on people again."

"Thanks for that, Molly," Hank said with genuine relief. "I believe we can make it if you and I are pulling in the same direction, but I think we need more help. How do we get it?"

The family continued talking. Sally protested that she didn't have a problem. Bobbie admitted that she thought Scott had a drug problem, but she denied vehemently that she was afraid to leave home. With a good deal of parental encouragement, Ryan talked about the parties at Roper's and about the accident with Zack.

Hank finally raised his arm. "Your mother and I need to talk. We have to address these issues one at a time. We'll all meet at breakfast to talk about this further."

Paul and Zack looked at each other. A small smile appeared on both their lips. Zack flashed Paul a "thumbs up" sign just as in the distance a loon gave its crazy call.

CHAPTER XVI

Paul's primary concern, as he lay in his bed in the dark that night, was the fact that Ryan lay in the bed right next to him, within easy striking distance. He knew by the irritated sighs and the restlessness that Ryan wasn't sleeping. He was afraid to ask Ryan what he was thinking, for fear of what the answer might be. Besides, Paul had done all the initiating he felt capable of for a while.

Suddenly, by the light coming in the window Paul saw Ryan's silhouette sit up. Paul cringed.

"There is a part of me that definitely wants to kick your butt, Paul," Ryan said.

Paul curled up in his bed, waiting for his brother to pounce.

"But you didn't let the family focus just on my

problem," Ryan continued from his bed, "which definitely would have happened if you hadn't said what you said. I appreciate that. So I'm going to wait to see what happens to me before I beat the snot out of you."

What a relief! Paul thought. I get to live—at least until tomorrow. Ryan lay back in his bed and the room fell silent again.

Paul then turned his attention next door. There was a continuous murmuring that Paul couldn't identify. A lot of it sounded angry, but just before he fell asleep he thought he heard a girlish sound that seemed only slightly like his mother's voice.

When he walked into the kitchen the next morning, Paul's suspicions were confirmed. There were his mother and father, hugging and looking at each other in a way they hadn't for a long time.

"Don't let me interrupt," he said with a grin.

His parents immediately opened their arms and invited him into their embrace. Somewhat awkwardly, he joined them. Being held by the two of them like this made him feel as safe as a baby, at least for the moment. Then Hank sat him down in a kitchen chair and took another across from him while Molly looked on.

"Paul," his dad said quietly. "You know I love sports, and especially football."

Paul nodded his head. Inside he groaned, thinking this was going to be another "Paul, you should be involved in sports" lecture.

"I thought the greatest thrill of my life was to watch your big brother Scott play," Hank said gently. "My favorite part of all was when we were waiting for the first kickoff and all the excitement of the game was in front of me. Then Scott would catch the ball and start running toward the other team. He would hurl himself full speed at the other team running at him full speed. I was so proud of him at that moment. I thought that was the most courageous thing I could ever see my kids do. I guess that's why it's never been a secret that I was disappointed when you and Ryan didn't follow in his footsteps."

Paul started to respond. His worst fears were being confirmed. He was a big disappointment to his father.

Hank interrupted before Paul could say anything. "Wait, Paul, hear me out. But when you did what you did yesterday, I realized that your action—though it will never make a trophy case—is the bravest thing I'll ever see one of my children do."

Paul tried to speak again but his father kept going. "As a matter of fact, Paul, your play last night is in another league from Scott's," Hank said earnestly. "If Scott were hurt being tackled, he would recover. It would only be a physical injury."

"But you risked a kind of injury from which you might never have recovered, Paul," Molly finished. "You ran full speed at the people who loved you and could have hurt you emotionally and spiritually. We're as proud of you as we could ever be of a child."

Paul rubbed the tears from his eyes and gave his mom and dad another hug. This is great, he thought.

Hank addressed the whole family at breakfast. "I guess I have to start with myself first," he said. "What Paul said last night made me realize how scared I am. I say I don't want to drink again—and I believe that! But I have to do my part to make that happen, and I haven't been. I have a new reason to go to meetings now, and I'll be there with a different attitude."

"Today, I'm going to call my sponsor and tell him about my slip at the party," Hank declared. "And I need to get started on that fourth step I've been putting off."

"I'm not as far along as your father," Molly interjected. "I have to work on my first step. But you can bet I'll be doing it."

"Now, as for the rest of you," Hank said firmly. All the children shifted uncomfortably in their chairs. "Ryan, you are grounded for a week, and your mother will be calling the other parents. Our main question is whether you have a serious problem with alcohol and drugs or are just experimenting, so we'll be taking you to the treatment center for an assessment."

"I don't think I've got a problem, but I'll go to talk to someone," Ryan answered quickly, sounding relieved at the relative lightness of the sentence.

"We'll all be there to support you—and also so that you don't minimize what you've done. I know all about doing that," Hank said with a rueful smile.

"Sally, you'll have to go for an assessment too," Hank said.

"Why me?" Sally shouted, jumping up. "I don't have a problem. I just wish you'd all leave me alone!"

"Sit down," Molly commanded. "Honey, we care too much about you to take that chance. We'll be with you."

Sally sat sullenly, glaring at Paul.

"We know these are hard things to hear—and hard changes to make," Hank said to his family. "But what Paul and Zack said to us last night was hard for them, too. We need to respect their courage and take a look at what they are saying to us. We need to love ourselves as much as they love us."

Everyone looked at Paul, who stared at his cereal.

"But there's one family problem we're not sure how to handle," Hank continued. "We're not sure what to do about Scott. I hate ignoring the problem, but I don't think we can order him to get help. And he has been so distant lately I don't think an intervention by us would have any impact."

Bobbie spoke up for the first time.

"I'm afraid that's true," she said. "I hope I'm not just making excuses for myself for not doing something before, but that's one of the reasons I haven't said anything to him. He's so angry at this family right now that I think anything we did or said right now would only make him angrier."

"There is something we can do that won't antagonize him," said Molly quietly. "We can get better ourselves . . . and pray for him."

Hank took Molly's hand and everyone grabbed the hand of the next person. For the first time in a long time, the Brandt family truly prayed together.

CHAPTER XVI

The following week was a busy one for the Brandts. Both assessments for Ryan and Sally took place, and the entire family was involved in each.

The counselors thought that, at the moment at least, Ryan was not addicted to either alcohol or drugs. He had definitely abused them both, however. The counselor suggested that, with their genetic predisposition towards alcoholism, probably none of Hank's children should drink.

Sally, on the other hand, definitely did have an eating disorder. They found an imbalance of salts and potassium in her body serious enough to require two days in the hospital. The counselor recommended both individual and family counseling. Sally still denied that she had a problem, however, and continued to vocally resist counseling.

Paul was sure that Sally and Ryan now hated him, but he had other things to worry about. Roper's parents had only grounded him for three days, and that sentence was now up. Today, as Paul kept close watch, the loon babies were getting their first swimming lesson. At first, they rode on their mother's back and she stayed close to the nest, but then she ventured further out.

Roper's grounding apparently had little effect, because he was sitting on his dock drinking beer with a bunch of guys. As soon as he saw the loons, he and his friends boarded his boat and headed for them.

"I'll show that little punk he shouldn't have ruined my summer," Roper declared to his friends as he headed full speed toward the nesting site.

The mother loon and her babies were several feet out from shore when Paul saw Roper's boat heading in their direction. The mother was in no danger. She could easily dive 200 feet, if need be, to avoid the boat. But the baby loons had not yet learned to swim, much less dive. They would float like corks to be churned by the propeller like eggs in a blender.

Paul moved into action instantly. He had already decided what he would do and he didn't waver now. He had gotten the idea from watching a nature program on how an environmental group saved whales from the whalers' harpoons.

He ran straight to the dinghy. He panicked when two pulls didn't start the small motor. Roper's boat was coming closer to the loons. On the third try, the motor finally caught. Paul quickly circled the dinghy between Roper and the loons.

When Roper saw Paul, his eyes brightened and he pushed the throttle all the way down, daring Paul to stay in his path. Paul could feel his heart pounding in his chest as the boat barreled towards him. It now became a battle of nerves.

Zack had stopped at the public beach on his way to the loon site just in time to observe Paul getting into position. There was no time to swim across the lake, and he knew no one would hear his cries over the roar of the engines.

Zack jumped into his car and headed toward the nesting site. He had to drive around the lake to get there, and he could only imagine what was happening from occasional glimpses through the trees.

Paul's eyes were closed, waiting for impact, when Roper finally turned aside. The wake from the large boat nearly turned the dinghy over. When Paul opened his eyes, he saw the big boat circling for another run at him. He noticed that the loons were safely ashore, and, not wanting to see if Roper would miss again, Paul turned his little boat toward shore. He purposely headed toward a spot away from where the loons had gone, and he reached the sand just as Roper's boat pulled in next to him.

Paul tried to run, but it was useless. Roper grabbed him before he had gotten ten feet. Paul struggled but was ineffective against Roper and his friends.

"You don't look so brave now, you little worm," Roper hissed. "Remember when I told you about that other grave we would have to dig? I'm not going to kill you, though, I've got a better idea." Roper turned to his friends. "Hey, let's throw him naked on the public beach!"

Somehow Roper knew that Paul despised his skinny body. Paul would skip gym just because he hated taking showers in front of others. The thought of being naked on a beach with people laughing made him sick. Paul also hated being held down. It reminded him of the times his brothers had done that to tease him when he was even smaller. He would sometimes dream of being trapped in a cave-in, and that same feeling of panic overwhelmed him now.

The boys had already pulled off Paul's shirt by the time Zack arrived.

"Leave him alone!" Zack yelled as he ran up.

"Oh, Zack, you've come to save your hero?" Roper mocked. "You're a little outnumbered, don't you think?" he laughed.

"You nearly killed me once, Roper," Zack said angrily, "I guess you'll get a second shot at it. The first time you had your boat. Now you're with your friends, but this time I'll get in at least one punch and count on the fact that it will land on your face."

"This is going to be even more fun than I thought!" Roper said with satisfaction. "We'll see how high and mighty you are when you and Paul are both naked on the beach. Too bad your friend Ryan isn't here," Roper replied as he and three of his friends left Paul and walked slowly toward Zack and began to circle him. "We could see whose side he would be on."

"With my brother and my best friend," a voice said from the woods. Ryan walked into the clearing with Sally, who had been swimming and had called home from the beach when she first saw Roper heading toward Paul.

When Ryan received Sally's call he tried to run immediately from the house, but Molly stopped him. "Where do you think you're going, young man?" she asked.

"Roper's after Paul," was all Ryan needed to say. Molly held out the car keys and told him to hurry.

Meanwhile, Sally had run the distance between the beach and the loon site in record time. She was just picking up a large stick when Ryan arrived. Brother and sister had silently looked at each other and then dashed toward the lake.

"So you're a Loonie now too, Ryan?" Roper said with a laugh. He had six friends with him, so he felt fairly confident. "A real bird lover. And speaking of birds, here's the whale turned stork," he said to Sally.

Sally glared at Roper and started toward him with the stick, but Ryan held her back.

"No, I don't care much about birds," Ryan said, looking at Paul's frightened eyes. Then his face softened, "But I love my brother and you're not going to hurt him," Ryan said firmly.

"Do you and your big jock friend and your little sister and brother really think you can stop all of us?" Roper said confidently.

"Well, we'll never find out big shot," Zack said, "because six of you have already left for that boat you like to aim at people."

Roper looked around anxiously to see his friends getting into the boat. "Just wait till you want something from me again," he said pointing at Ryan and starting to back away.

Ryan grabbed Paul's torn shirt from Roper's hands and Roper jumped. He then ran toward his boat.

Roper was climbing into the boat when another voice came from the woods. "Just a minute, young man," Mark Jones called as he walked toward Roper.

"What do you want, wimp?" Roper called as he

climbed into his boat.

Mr. Jones walked up to Paul. "Are you all right?" he asked.

Paul nodded his head.

"Sorry I haven't been here for a while, but I didn't abandon you or the loons," Mr. Jones said gently. "I've been busy."

The teacher then walked into the water with his shoes and socks still on so he could get just inches from Roper's face. "I just wanted to let you know, Mr. Roper, that this area is now approved by the State Department of Natural Resources as a wildlife preserve," he said loudly, "and if I see you or your friends over here again, I'll have you arrested. Second, I know a reporter who is doing a story on alcohol abuse and boating and she's very interested in the true story of what happened to Zack. I think publicity might finally get your parents' attention about you. I'm also going to add today's incident to the pot. Now get out of here."

The snarl on Roper's face was replaced by a look of fear. He started the boat engine and sped off.

Ryan turned to Paul and handed him his shirt. He put his arm around his little brother's bare shoulders, which were suddenly not quite so burdened.

"Let's go see those loons you're so crazy about," Ryan said with a big smile. He put his other arm around Zack and said simply, "Thanks."

Sally walked to the other side and added her arm to Paul's shoulders. "Yeah," she said. "Let's get close and see if the chicks follow Paul or their mother."

Everyone, including Mr. Jones, laughed. Paul just smiled.

CHAPTER XVIII

"Let's go, Brandts! It's cold out here," Zack yelled as he ran in place outside their house.

Soon Ryan, Sally, and Paul appeared on the porch in their running gear. The friends all took off for the lake. It was late autumn now, and they had been back in school for a few months. The bond between Ryan and Zack had become stronger, and Ryan no longer was hanging out with Roper and his gang. As a matter of fact, Ryan was trying out for the swim team. He was getting a late start as a senior, but he and Zack were running each morning and swimming in the pool each afternoon. Zack was sure Ryan would at least make some of the relay teams.

This morning, as usual, the two teenagers ran a little faster than Sally and Paul and were soon well ahead of them. They joked and laughed with each other as they pulled away down the road.

Paul and Sally followed. They began running together again after the incident with Roper. Sally was still having trouble with her eating disorder, but her parents encouraged her to continue to run and participate in other sports because they knew it was one thing that really helped her feel better about herself. She was eating more regularly, and part of her therapy was to help her mother do the grocery shopping.

Nothing had changed in Scott's life, as far as anyone knew, but the family always included him in the prayer they now shared each night before dinner. Molly told Pastor Brooks in one of their frequent visits that she thought God was the most successful therapist anyway.

One of Paul's biggest surprises had come on one of the last days of summer, when his mother visited him at the loon site. She brought a lunch for the two of them and stayed most of the day. "I forgot how peaceful nature allows me to be," she said as she sat sunning herself and watching the four loons swim.

Bobbie kept the family informed about Scott after her visits to his college to see her boyfriend, Tom. She was visiting nearly every weekend now and had already applied to attend the same college herself the following semester.

As for Paul, he was still much the same, but he was slowly becoming more outgoing. Sally was still his best friend, and Mr. Jones was still his favorite teacher. One day, Mark Jones brought a date to a junior high basketball game at school. Paul caught his attention as they sat in the stands, then folded his arms like a praying mantis. Mr. Jones laughed and turned to his date.

"I think I just saw a praying mantis in the hall," he said slyly to his woman friend. "Did I ever tell you about their mating practices?"

"Several times," she said with a smile.

Roper never bothered the loons again, but that didn't mean they were out of danger. Because they were hatched so late, there was a chance they wouldn't learn to fly before the lake froze for the long Wisconsin winter. Loons are very heavy birds for their size. That weight is a great help in diving but a liability during takeoffs. And, since they don't nest in trees, the young have to learn the difficult art of taking off from the lake: a long, hard run across the water with wings flapping vigorously before eventual take off.

It had been a long and beautiful fall, but the leaves had now fallen and a skim of ice was appearing on the lake during the long nights. If the young loons couldn't take off soon, the lake would freeze over and they would die.

Paul was nervous as he and Sally approached the lake this morning for fear it had frozen over solid during the cold night. As they approached the lake, they saw Zack and Ryan jumping up and down and waving their arms. Paul and Sally sprinted to see what the commotion was about. They arrived just in time to see the two young loons, side by side, finish their long runs and clear the water for their first flight.

Paul, Sally, Ryan and Zack hugged one another. The loons might have to stop at several other lakes along their flight south to warmth and safety, but they'd make it now. Paul felt like a proud parent who drops his child off at school for the first time. He knew that his brother, the loon, would return next spring.

"You know, Paul," said Sally, as they walked home together, "you've had quite a summer. You've saved two loons and two people. You can be very proud of yourself."

"Two people?" Paul asked, confused.

"Yes. Zack . . . and me," she said. She put her hand on his shoulder. "Thanks, brother," she said sweetly. Then she punched him in the stomach and took off running home.

Paul followed, running like the loons flew. He was aware of his feet touching the ground for a few more steps, but after that he was soaring.

Acknowledgments

You'll have to forgive me. I know that acknowledgments are just supposed to give credit to the people who helped you write a book, but in a way all these people did help me write it. But, in addition, publishing a book is such a rare opportunity that it is difficult to pass up the chance to thank people who have affected my life, and not just this book.

Everybody should have an Aunt Antoinette. From the time I was little I remember her telling stories about me, my brothers and sister, and my cousins. I heard each of those stories dozens of times, but each time she'd tell one of them her eyes would sparkle and her laughter overflow with love. I don't know if she is where I got my appreciation for stories, but Antoinette certainly helped me know that I am loved not only by her but by my whole extended family.

Another supportive family of mine has been the staff and students at the College of DuPage. I was only twenty-four years old when I started there, and it seems like I grew up there professionally. Tom Richardson and I fit together like a couple in a good marriage. He picked up on the things that I was not good at or didn't like. Through the years, the students and staff have been so nurturing and supportive that I started doing things I never thought I could—like writing stories. I have received lots of help on this one from Rosemary McKinney, Frank Salvatini, Frances Roshier and Lin Bresnahan. They not only were early readers, but taught me a lot about addiction, recovery and eating disorders. Barb Marsh and Judy Czarapata also contributed suggestions and friendship. Cheri Erdman, Rosalyn Long and Beth Ellis read early versions and took the time to not only support me but to suggest specific changes that I made. Beth Ellis and Pat Bodrava helped with typing and Bill Makely with editing.

Several students helped, too. Gretchen Puglies, Marlene Fratus, Lydia Wilder, Rita Sullivan, Charlene Keane and Elizabeth O'Flynn read the book and gave me support. Rich Weigel and David Lloyd also read the book, but most of all they provided me with positive models of young people with wisdom beyond their years.

All along I felt God was there. That was never more evident than last Christmas when I was getting more and more frustrated with how slowly the rewriting and editing was going. Just then Joanne Kutner called and asked me how I was doing. When I shared my frustration, she offered to help and just happened to know well the computer program I was using. A day later my problems were solved.

And finally, thanks to Greg Pierce, my editor at ACTA Publications, who spent endless hours with this book and told me the painful things I needed to hear to make it work.

Also by Robert Bollendorf

If you enjoyed this story of the Brandt family, you'll also want to read *Sober Spring: One Family's Battle with Addiction* by Robert Bollendorf. *Sober Spring* tells of the efforts of Molly Brandt and her children to confront Hank Brandt about his alcoholism.

ISBN: 0-915388-32-4; 166 pp, $5.95
Available through most bookstores or by calling 800-397-2282.

"Robert Bollendorf brings hope to families who feel hopelessly caught in the bondage of alcoholism. *Sober Spring* captures the array of emotions in individual experiences when considering an intervention. Above all, it dramatically expresses a truth that every alcoholic family needs to know—intervention works!"

—Dennis Morreim
Author, *The Road to Recovery*

"In novel form, *Sober Spring* puts the reader into the mental, physical, and spiritual shoes of the afflicted and affected victims of alcoholism. The family nature of this illness is shown in each member's emotional involvement in denial, identification, intervention, treatment and ongoing recovery. This book deserves to be in the libraries of all people helpers."

—The Rev. Phil Hansen
Abbott Northwestern Hospital
Minneapolis

I find *Sober Spring* engaging, insightful, and helpful. It should be a welcome addition to the intervention process."

—The Rev. Carl Anderson
Parkside Medical Services, Inc.

Sober Spring is witness to the human tragedies, the pain, the sorrow of chemical dependency. It is also witness to the joy and the hope that comes with treatment."

—Rita L. Bobrowski, M.S., C.A.A.C.
Coordinator/Director,
Addictions Counselor
Training Program
College of DuPage

"I recommend *Sober Spring* for those experienced clinical practitioners who have made it beyond the panicked search for techniques in this field—as a reminder of the real risks involved in change. For those still engaged in that search, it is required reading."

—David J. Clark, PHD., S.C.A.C.
Co-director,
GIFT Training Institute

"One gets the sense from *Sober Spring* of the range of feelings and frustrations that not only the alcoholic but also the family and loved ones go through in dealing with this deadly disease. It clearly points out that there is no 'bad guy' and paints a picture of the warm personalities and real people that are involved."

—Joseph E. Triani, M.A., C.A.C.
Administrator,
CAREUNIT of DuPage

"*Sober Spring* belongs in the hands of all who work with hurting people, who have situations in the home which require confrontation, and anyone who has a desire to understand and help in the healing process of those who come into their lives."

—Regis Walling
Upper Peninsula Catholic